Roots, Branches and Buzz Saws
More Stories of August Kibler

Dear Reader:
This book has been written with the assumption that
you have first read *As the Daisies Bloom* which introduces
many of the characters, and describes how
their lives are woven into August's life. However, many
other characters in *Roots, Branches and Buzz Saws*
are new and have their own story to tell. Hopefully,
it is a compelling story in its own right.

Dedicated to the remnant
living peaceably and in hope
for what *can* be.

Writings of T.P. Graf

As the Daisies Bloom - A Novel

PenCraft Awards - 2020 First Place, Cultural Fiction
Book Excellence Awards - 2021 Finalist, Friendship
Chanticleer IBA, 2020 First Place, Somerset Book Awards

A beautiful telling of life's trials and tribulations, always overcome by the love of family and of something greater than oneself. - Reader's Favorite

Enchanting as it is charming ... intimately and poetically told ... like a well-written symphony - Literary Titan

A powerfully written character-led novel; stark and unsettling but often funny too. Highly recommended! - A 'Wishing Shelf' Book Review

August Kibler's Stories for Tyler
Voices of Context from Eden to Patmos
(Companion to As the Daisies Bloom)

Firebird Award - 2021 Winner, Christian Poetry
American Book Awards - 2021 Finalist, Religious Poetry
Royal Dragonfly, 2021 Honorable Mention, Religion/Spirituality

A compelling and thought-provoking study of the bible and Christian history. The writing style is almost angelic! It's the sort of book you want to discuss; that stays with you for a long, long time.
- A 'Wishing Shelf' Book Review

Graf has crafted a masterful work of modern literature that takes on some very complex topics...in a format that any reader can engage with and glean wisdom from ... entertaining ... highly recommend.
- Reader's Favorite

The book offers fresh ideas ... absorbing ... thought-provoking and evokes a positive emotional connotation. - Literary Titan

Roots, Branches and Buzz Saws
More Stories of August Kibler

"Celebrate who you are, even if it is quietly...". That is what this book is, a celebration of August's life and a reminder to the reader to celebrate their life, who they are. - Literary Titan

This book is a perfect example of how each life is valuable and is a story to tell…
important … impactful … perfect slice-of-life novel
- Readers' Favorite

Insightful, powerful, a story of life and how it's changed by so many tiny
happenings. Highly recommended! - A 'Wishing Shelf' Book Review

Looking Out onto Our World
Explorations of Power, Dogma and
a World Deserving of Contemplation

Insightful, intelligent; the sort of poetry that will stay with you for a long time.
Highly recommended. - A 'Wishing Shelf' Book Review

Alive with sensory experience…refusing standard conventions
of storytelling…confident…each word in each verse deliberate …
arranged for maximum impact…ripping and compelling …
will engage even the most reluctant poetry reader. - Literary Titan

Introspective … thoughtful and fascinating a realistic observation
of life's journey … with an eye towards hope and celebration …
full of emotive and intelligent wordplay … highly recommended …
a great pick me up and talking point to share with others.
- Reader's Favorite

The Life and Stories of Jaime Cruz (Trilogy)

Chanticleer IBA, 2021 Finalist, Laramie Book Awards:
TP Graf for a Series - Americana Western Fiction
International Impact Book Awards, Winner, TP Graf - Author for a Series
Chanticleer IBA, 2022 Finalist - Book Series Award

Tumbleweed and Dreams (Book One)
From the Series - The Life and Stories of Jaime Cruz

Firebird Award - 2021 Winner, Book in a Series
Firebird Award - 2021 Winner, Multicultural Fiction
American Fiction Awards - 2021 Finalist, Multicultural Fiction
Hollywood Book Festival - 2021 Honorable Mention, General Fiction
Book Excellence Awards - 2023 Finalist, Multicultural Fiction

Graf manages to keep readers enthralled with Jaime's day-to-day experiences chapter after chapter ... a beautifully penned tale of self-discovery and a strong main character who stands out in a crowd.
- Literary Titan

A gripping story filled with colorful and often captivating characters.
- A 'Wishing Shelf' Book Review

An immersive journey of self-discovery and a sense of home ... you find yourself invested in the lives of the people and the friendships that are made. - Readers' Favorite

Night Air Descending (Book Two)
From the Series - The Life and Stories of Jaime Cruz

A cleverly-crafted, character-led family drama set in Texas. I got so immersed in it, I started to feel like one of the family too!
- A 'Wishing Shelf' Book Review

Whether you're in the mood for a slice-of-life drama or a study of eclectic characters, Night Air Descending by T.P. Graf is a memorable read.
- Readers' Favorite

This is a beautifully written book that has a grounded and authentic feel so much that it feels like we are reading someone's diary ... heartwarming ... [with a] distinct literary aesthetic. - Literary Titan

Seeds in the Desert Wind (Book Three)
From the Series - The Life and Stories of Jaime Cruz

Every quirk, every nuance, and each daily challenge make this story relatable and enjoyable...a book that wraps around you like your favorite blanket and touches your heart in a unique way. - Literary Titan

Graf again delivers interesting, full-bodied characters that we can relate to and want to follow through to their conclusions... a story that will entertain and move you. - Readers' Favorite

A powerful, often thought-provoking end to this excellent trilogy. Highly recommended. - A 'Wishing Shelf' Book Review

A Cowgirl's Stories
Companion to The Life and Stories of Jaime Cruz Trilogy

Days in the Desert
Food for Body and Soul

Table of Contents

August's File 1

A Precarious Start 4

Hope Mennonite 18

Marching Off to War 41

School Days 45

Guide of Soul and Mind 74

Union, Justice, and Confidence......................100

Life in the Mountains 139

Building House and Home...............................162

Talking Politics at the Table...........................191

What Was and Is 205

August's File

Prologue

As August's executor, I really had little to do. His generosity to us and a few others—one niece, Noel, Ethel and Maggie—were taken care of in his good planning without any need to probate his estate. He was also not a collector of things—or if he ever was, he'd thinned them down before we ever met him. If he had taken many pictures over the years, he must have either sent some to relatives or friends or disposed of them. Christian and I found nothing to indicate any photo history of his life other than a few on his computer which came back to us from the cruise line about the same time his ashes arrived.

Christian said, "Maybe he liked the Amish notion—'make no graven image'—and thus didn't take many pictures."

I said, "That might well be part of it. The other part being, his mind could hold onto beauty and any moment in time that was meaningful to him as though it had been recorded on film. To him, the words he recorded for us were his way of filling in the blanks that a collection of pictures could never provide."

I knew he read a lot, but I also knew he had a habit of giving books away about as soon as he'd finish one. He kept a few that I will always keep and share with the boys—ones where he has color tags hanging all over the book, marking things he clearly liked. I was surprised that a couple were pretty heavy reading on philosophy which he would have never let on as something within his "intellectual capacity." I truly believe he regarded himself as a mediocre student but was certainly honest in his love of life-long learning. For us on that front, he was on par with Momma and Pappy for passing along all life had taught him.

What I did find of interest on the computer, with his high security password, "penny-girl,"was a collection of writings which clearly were put down over time and mostly predated our time in his life—some of which he seems to have culled previously to include in the work he had done for Johnny and Jimmy. There, he had included enough to account for some of his life with Miles particularly, their time in Boone, but little of his childhood or a more in-depth account of their lives together. I have no idea how long he might have been working on these recollections, but it was clear he had done so right up to the end as the last file date was the day he emailed me to say he had the virus. I thought it was probably then, in his mischievous self, that he added that password. Christian and I, having been appointed executors, had a list of his important accounts which he kept in a small safe, and every single account had a different and highly secure password—the kind that is supposed to take two million years to crack. His deliberate use of "penny-girl" strongly suggested to me that he smiled while "securing" the file. I also thought, surely he must be putting these together to someday hand me yet another three-ring binder of his stories.

As our friends and family in Boone, Columbia and Macon learned of the stories he'd done for us, we all began to share them more widely. With this in mind, I am making this collection available to anyone interested as well. Here we see the earlier years when he wasn't the old man, as he so fondly referred to himself in the years we knew him. He kept these under the file name *Roots, Branches and Buzz Saws.* I have no idea how he came up with that name—he never says—but like August, it somehow exemplifies his willingness to trim away the dead wood needed to keep the good tree healthy.

August was a lover of trees. He shared with us how, as a boy, he frequently replanted seedlings from the woods on their farm. How with each death in the family, he and his mother would go to the woods to find another tree for the cemetery. He expressed to us his lifelong admiration for their deep roots and beautiful structure, and how that beauty and grace would be extended into a second life as a fine timber frame building or a well-built piece of furniture.

Maybe he would have gotten around to explaining the file name if given the chance to work on it longer—though it certainly appears he was making an end. However, it strikes me as a fitting metaphor for his life, and that perhaps was his intention.

The only surprise to me was that he'd never mentioned these writings. I assume if he'd not wanted me to share them, he would have put in all caps at the beginning, "Tyler—DO NOT DISTRIBUTE!" Since he did not and since he did make me his executor, it seems right that I preserve and share them for any interested.

Tyler Ethen Marvel-Jemison
Boone, North Carolina
13 December 2020

A Precarious Start

Chapter One

My mother was from firm stock. It is important to know this to have even the vaguest notion of the kind of childhood I had. This was true both in her physical stature and her temperament. We seem to be from a long line of average height, above average muscular build and no-nonsense ancestors. Certainly, Mom shared these traits. I can imagine she could have had twelve children and been no worse for wear. Other factors would see to it that her family was smaller than these of her ancestors. She should have quit before she got to me as she carried the Rh negative antibodies —my father being Rh positive. Her doctor warned her to be prepared for the worst when the time of my birth came. Back in those days, death or severe brain damage were possible—even expected—for children born further up the chronological chain than I as her fourth child.

It's odd that I never thought to ask her, when I finally learned this before she died, whether she ever revealed the doctor's warning to my dad. It wouldn't have surprised me in the least if this was something she carried on her own. She was not one to share her pain with others. Nor was she ever to be accused of selfishness or self pity. I would go so far as to say, sympathy and sentimentality were foreign concepts to her—traits, whether intentional or not, she seems to have passed on to me in a stronger measure than her other children. Maybe she was toughening me up knowing the precarious start I had in this world.

What I did know about my birth was that I had a blood transfusion because of Rh factor. I even knew the blood donor's name, Jordie Thompson. His wife, Blanche, was a nurse in the delivery room, and she knew her husband was a match and called him "to hightail it to the hospital." I just didn't have a clue as a child, or much of my adult life, that such a thing was as life threatening and dangerous as it actually was. I've wondered, but never asked, if she gave herself the space to detach a bit from her pregnancy with me in case the worst did happen. I have to think she did. Who wouldn't?

I only learned the rest of the story when I shared with her my trouble with a minister from my childhood who had been to an evangelical university and was convinced that if we didn't know the day and the hour we "accepted Jesus," then we weren't "saved." I told him I'd always believed. He only reiterated his born-again stand—making me feel rather dense and small in the process. I added in my telling to her something I wished I'd had the wisdom to say to him all those years ago. I said, "What a sad reflection on the heritage of a mother's faith to say that a child can't be instilled with faith from the womb." And with that she shared, with her now forty-something-year-old son, her story of putting me in God's hands. I guess I was her miracle baby. She did have sense enough to quit after me. How she ensured that, I cannot say.

That minster would fall far heavier on the fundamentalist scale than I would ever fall myself. It seems a great inconsistency to me that the church "dedicated" babies when they first came with their mothers to church. Apparently, the gift to God of our life wasn't a real thing at that point—at least in his limited view or more accurately the view of his limited god. You had to be a teenager before Jesus would come into your heart and then only by invitation. So much for being created in the image and likeness of the Creators. (See Genesis 1:26 if you think using the plural is heresy.) I believe what "saves" us is present from our first breath. Life's journey is finding that which nurtures us. You can call that our "soul" or our "salvation" or whatever term works for you. It doesn't change the inherent gift of joy and gratitude within us.

My mother, Katherine "Katie" Shudel, was from a big family of Swiss Mennonites—though there was some wandering back and forth into Alsace. Her dad, Johannes Jacob Shudel, was a farmer and timber framer—building many barns in the county where they lived in northern Ohio. Her mother, Marie Koenig, emigrated when she was a teenager with her family. My mother was a lot like Grandma Marie in looks, stature and temperament. Grandma was always rattling things off in her Swiss-German dialect. If I didn't know better, I'd have said she was talkin' dirty, but I know she wasn't. I just wish she'd have had her children and grandchildren learn to be multilingual, as she and Grandpa both were.

Grandma Shudel always said she'd never been stung by a bee her entire life. When she was a small child, they would land on her and she would just look at them. After she and Grandpa settled on the farm, she kept several bee hives and never wore any protective gear—didn't even own a beekeeper's suit or use smoke to settle the bees. To us kids she claimed, "The bees and I have a bargain. As long as I keep my children and grandchildren in line, the bees promise they won't sting me."

While we doubted her claim, we couldn't deny there was some mutual bond between her and those bees. Maybe it was her ear boxing us that kept her safe all those years. I've been stung by a wasp a time or two but never by a bee. Maybe she'd instructed them to leave me be as long as I didn't misbehave too badly.

She was meticulous caring for the hives, which meant different tasks according to the seasons of the year. One day, when I was about nine or ten, Mom and I were tagging along as she made her way to the orchard where she kept the hives. We stood back a ways as she opened up the boxes to check on her bees.

I said to Mom, "Where did Grandma learn to keep bees?"

Mom said, "I asked her that when I was about your age, and she told me the bees told her what they wanted and she just followed their orders. I think it probably had more to do with one of those French or German books she has in the house she knew I couldn't read. You know she likes to pull your leg when she gets a chance."

Chapter Two

My clearest memory of Grandpa Shudel is from a few months before his death when I went with him to his workshop, and he set me up on his workbench. He got a piece of scrap timber and showed me how he would use all the different hand tools that had been passed on to him from his dad—block planes, chisels, brace and bits, draw knives, hand augers, rip saws and others. Then he made a mortise and grabbed another piece to make a tenon, put them together, handed me the hand auger and said I should drill out a hole in one particular spot. He had to do the real work, of course—going on six at the time, I wasn't strong enough to drill out the wood. Then he picked up an oak peg and one of his wooden mallets and had me drive the peg in to secure the mortise and tenon together. That I could do, though it took quite a few strokes to do it. I remember looking up at him with a big smile on my face from my accomplishment.

He smiled back and said, "Sehr gut," and added, "That's what your great-grandpa would have said. It means very good. We might be able to make a carpenter out of you if we keep after it long enough."

Grandpa liked to write poems, though it seemed to be for him more an exercise of putting his thoughts on paper than wanting to share them with the world. Mom remembers him scribbling these from when she was little enough to still sit on his lap. They were written on scraps of paper and left lying around in drawers or in books as book marks. Very few survived past his own lifetime which Mom blamed on one particularly careless sibling going through his things when he died and mindlessly tossing them out with other "trash."

Mom had one of Grandpa's poems, which she copied for all of us and gave to us when we graduated from high school:

Post and Beam

The oak I milled this morning,
cut from the north woods
a season ago, left drying,

had rings that betrayed
its quiet record of time.
Ninety-five years, patient,
no rushing in its seasons.

I picked up my father's old block plane—
now in my own hands as I press hard
to chamfer the corners of the post
as it enters its second life
for some fine building with
the promise of another
ninety-five years or more.

My father taught me to press
the plane down hard on the wood
to shave it smooth. He told me,
good work requires a strong and
steady hand, patient always
for the beauty good work ensures.

With the old augur, I drilled each corner
for the mortise—then the chisel
from his tools met his hammer
to chip away the joinery paired in
perfect dimension to its tenon in
the beam cut from the same oak.

The care of tools and wood
and men are in all ways
how we show our love to God—
never rushed or discarded in anger.
Crafted to last for generations.
Always to honor what can be.

When Grandpa Shudel died, perhaps because he died on my sixth birthday, Grandma gave me his Bible, which has such small print you about need a magnifying glass to read it—he must have had good vision. Folded up inside and tucked in the Beatitudes in Matthew was another of his poems.

Dove of Peace

It takes strength to control the hand
of one so bent to his own command
as the poor languish from his demand
unable to ever truly stand
within a warring and battered land

The men strike out in fear and hate
knowing regrets that prove too late
failing to alter their bitter fate
as they punish those of lesser state
in ongoing acts that never abate

The dove of peace hovers ever near
patiently waiting from year to year
for hearts working for peace to appear
ending malice that proved so severe
alas rejoicing, drying each tear

I've never been sure what to do with the Bible. With no children of my own, I need to give it to someone or at least let Tyler and Christian know what to do with it. I suppose the best thing would be to see if the niece, who has been my health directive power of attorney all these years, wants it. If she doesn't want it, I'd just as soon the Marvel-Jemisons keep it. Why this one procrastination persists of my Last Will and Testament is a bit of a mystery. I guess I've just been reluctant to pass it on, as I'm certain it can't mean to the next recipient what it has meant to me all these years. Given this attachment, I must, after all, have at least one drop of sentimentality that my unsentimental mother perhaps didn't have—though she had her own keepsakes, so I suspect she had a bit more sentimentality than she let on. And as I get older and cry more easily, I find, too, I must have more than I ever allowed my mind to think I had.

Grandma and Grandpa Shudel knew well the precarious start of trying to bring up children. Infant mortality and childhood illness being what they were, and large families in those days being what they were, they had six of eight children live to adulthood. One boy would die at birth and the other, a girl, died when she was about two.

It is probably all in my imagination but I think looking back, Grandma Shudel had a certain fondness for me—perhaps for having beaten the odds of my own precarious birth. I speculate, if Mom had confided in just one other person about the doctor's warning, I believe it would have been her mother.

I had great admiration for our family doctor—the one who brought me into this world and had warned my mother of my possible fate. Being ignorant about my birth beyond my transfusion, it never occurred to me that on my doctor's visits he might have looked at me a bit differently than most of his other child patients. And I suspect he didn't. However, I do recall on every visit when he would enter the small exam room his eyes would be bright, and he would smile and seem to have all the time in the world. He also was a surgeon and operated on me twice over the years for minor things—once when I managed to step on a spike which went deep into my foot and once to have my appendix removed. Despite my admiration for him, that never translated to admiration for any other doctor, it must be said. I would never go to another doctor unless absolutely necessary which, so far, I have never had to do.

I did learn as an adult that he was the first doctor anywhere around who would perform an abortion when the law allowed. It made me wonder—if the law had allowed in early 1956 when my mother first went to see him to confirm her pregnancy, would he have suggested she abort? From all I've gathered about him, it seemed that any such decision would be the woman's to make—not one he imposed in any fashion. I suspect my mother would have risked it. It might seem odd that as I was reflecting on this, my mind went immediately to Jeremiah who lamented his birth and wondered why God didn't abort him. Of course, our Bibles don't use that term, but if one can read Jeremiah 20 and cast it in any other light, I'd like to know how. Well, I never cursed my birth or the doctor who brought me forth—though I did curse moments of my life plenty of times.

Chapter Three

The Kiblers were also Swiss Mennonites and my great-grandfather, Henri, emigrated as a boy and married Magdalena Schneiter from another family who emigrated at the same time as the Kiblers. Henri and Magdalena settled on a farm next to the Shudels. Their boys, including my grandpa, Christian, would take up the mason trade which Henri also knew—his father even built a protestant stone church in Switzerland and another in Alsace before emigrating—and were known to put in the foundations for the barns my grandpa Shudel would raise with the neighborhood crew.

His mother's family, the Schneiters, was from across the border in Alsace—also Mennonite or as they were often referred to at the time, Amish Mennonite. Great-great-grandma Schneiter used to get hauled out of their home in the village to translate for the local German command during the Franco-Prussian War. Somehow they figured out that she was perfectly bilingual in German and French —knowing all the local dialects—and that was all the excuse they needed. It wasn't long after the war they came to America. She would then learn her third language. Great-grandpa Kibler clearly knew French as my dad recalled him subscribing to a French newspaper all his life. Dad attributed this attachment to French to the fact that his Swiss dialect was pretty far from high German and French was just easier to read.

By the time I came along, most of the ancestors were gone—the result of being the youngest child of the youngest child for a couple of generations on both sides.   I never knew any of my great-grandparents or my paternal grandfather. My other grandparents were all gone before I was old enough for high school. We did have a large extended family of three generations, and my mother excelled at keeping everyone straight on her side of the family.

Whether out of lack of interest or family-tree overload, Mom never bothered to record in her mind (or paper) Dad's side of the family as she had her own. Dad wasn't much help in that regard either, even though we lived on the "old Kibler homestead."

A few basic things I knew. Dad was the youngest son of Christian Kibler and Ursula Leichti. He was never fond of his name

—especially his middle name. His mother was from a long line of fathers whose name was Hieronimus. Dad was named after the old-world names that never quite got updated—Georg Hieronimus. He spent his life dealing with the misspelling of Georg and hoping against hope he didn't have to spell out that middle name. The oldest brother, Christian, lucked into getting named from the Kibler side of the family. Dad's only consolation was the fact that at least that old Leichti name was his middle name and not his first.

Dad told Mom when they married, "I don't want to saddle any of our children with old family names in some attempt to honor them."

Thus it was Mom and Dad's first three children had simple "American" names of the current day—Wayne Lee, Deb Marie, and Kathy Sue. Deb wasn't even Deborah. By the time I came along, Grandpa Kibler had died a year earlier. This prompted him to relent a bit with his last child, and they named me after my great-grandfather, August Koenig, Grandma Shudel's father, and Dad's grandfather, Henri Kibler. While Georg Hieronimus never liked his name, August Henri loved his. I appreciated both the family connection and the fact it was a bit from the norm of the day. That said, I wouldn't have wanted to honor the family line by extending Hieronimus into another generation.

Beyond that, there was little I knew of our family history. Dad was certainly a "family first" man, and so I never quite reconciled his lack of sharing his family's history with his children.

Maybe it runs in the blood. When I did ancestry work I couldn't see that my siblings or cousins were much interested even though in digging into it, I dispelled more than one family myth about our origins. The most obvious myth was that most of my Kibler cousins told people they were from Germany when, in fact, going back a few hundred years they were Swiss through and through—not just the Kiblers themselves but except for the few Alsatians thrown in and some moving back and forth across the border, everyone in the family tree was Swiss. (I assume they were after some new blood when they looked in Alsace). After two world wars with Germany, I'm not sure how that German label stuck, but it did. I'd have thought to be Swiss or French would have been a plus.

13

I wish I had more tangible pearls of wisdom from these generations before me. I know they were peaceable and prosperous —not in some materialistic accumulation but rather a generosity of spirit and neighborliness that is increasingly lacking in my generation. I am reminded of the Edwin Muir poem, *The Good Town*, where he instructs us of the work that is required each generation.

How could our town grow wicked in a moment?
What is the answer? Perhaps no more than this,
That once the good men swayed our lives, and those
Who copied them took a while the hue of goodness,
A passing loan; while now the bad are up,
And we, poor ordinary neutral stuff,
Not good nor bad, must ape them as we can,
In sullen rage or vile obsequiousness.
…when evil comes
All things turn adverse, and we must begin
At the beginning, heave the groaning world
Back in its place again, and clamp it there.

I can say for certain, too many depend on the goodness to pass along in some optimistic preordination. Muir is right—we must begin again. Yes, for every generation and for every baby born, it is a precarious start.

Chapter Four

As a child looking at the Kibler farm and all the farms in our township it seemed as though these picture-perfect, idealized Midwestern landscapes had somehow been this way for centuries. They are, of course, recent additions. The township had its first homesteaders in the 1830s. All my ancestors arrived between 1834 and 1876—Johnny-come-lately's compared to the African Americans brought by force to this country.

On both the Kibler and Shudel sides of my family, I had multigenerational ancestors who brought their large families and were among the first to settle in our township. The Shudels and other Amish-Mennonite families traveled from their homes by hiring wagons to transport them to Le Havre, France, which in itself was a seventeen-day trip. They waited there two weeks for a vessel. From there they sailed for New York on a long and tedious seven-week voyage. As tedious as it was, it was without incident and all who departed Le Havre arrived alive and well in New York. These were large families with as many as twelve children. Clearly, the formidable stock of my mother came by her honestly.

The Kiblers traveled in style by comparison. They were on a larger ship which left after their Amish-Mennonite brethren and arrived before them. All met up in Ohio at an established Amish-Mennonite community before heading further west to find land they could homestead. A guide led them to our unsettled township where they decided to stake their claim. It was described in family lore as "wild and dreary" with "rich soil."

As prescribed by the Land Ordinance of 1785, Ohio had platted the land into square mile sections—each section thus consisting of 640 acres with 36 sections comprising a township. Each section was then platted into 80-acre tracts for homesteading. It was all very orderly compared to the more free form boundaries of their homeland, shaped more by the landscape than the Jeffersonian lines superimposed on a map.

All these beautiful farms of my childhood were carved out carefully and laboriously by my ancestors as they cleared some for tillable land and dug drainage ditches to transform swampy soils into rich and fertile fields—always preserving a healthy portion of mostly undisturbed woodlands on their 80-acre tracts of land. There was no subservient labor involved—it was all neighbor helping neighbor. They milled their own timber and built homes, barns and other outbuildings to support their livelihood and raise their children.

Those early generations seemed to have an inherent knowledge of the importance of wetlands that later generations would fight to eliminate—trying to expand their tillable land. For many, this was a losing battle but not one conceded without years of trying. Those who did succeed created the large fields easily joined with adjacent land to create the flat, monoculture corn and soy bean fields that have become the ubiquitous reality of farms across the Midwest. Progress, some would call it, and the kind of progress the "get-big-or-get-out" government liked to subsidize.

Switzerland has long maintained mandatory conscription for military service even though the last time they were under some degree of foreign control by another state, France, was in the early 1800s. The French finally left after they were tired of dealing with the uncooperative Swiss. The last "war" they fought was in 1845. Several conservative Catholic cantons formed an alliance to launch a civil war against their more protestant, federally aligned fellow citizens. The war lasted from November 3 to November 29, and claimed fewer than one hundred lives. The general who led the federal alliance ordered his men to retrieve and care for all injured from the rebel forces.

Conscription wasn't the sole reason for my Mennonite ancestors leaving when they did. The harsher persecution of the earlier years of the Reformation when they were killed for their "radical" beliefs had largely passed. Their large agrarian families needed land to farm, and in those days Switzerland was still a very poor nation—landlocked and lacking any natural resources or foreign conquests that brought wealth as they had to neighboring countries. It seems ironic that my peaceable ancestors should leave there to come to a nation where they could register as conscientious objectors but whose government would continue a long history of going from war to war to war.

The rich soils of their northern Ohio farms would help them prosper, but their life wasn't without economic downturns. My Grandma Shudel told me about Grandpa milking cows before he had much help to do it from their growing children. It was the height of the depression and an unemployed man had wandered onto the farm looking for work and a place to stay.

Grandpa told him, "I can't pay any regular wages. All we can provide is a bed and food to eat."

The man took the work, the bed and the food. Still Grandpa tried to pay him something as bills would allow. Grandma remembers one Saturday where all Grandpa had left from paying the bills was twenty-five cents. He reached in his pocket and placed the two dimes and five pennies in the man's hand.

To the man all he said was, "I'm sorry it can't be more."

Hope Mennonite

Chapter Five

I really wish I'd had the good fortune of knowing all my grandparents—while I grew up and into my adulthood. They were more than just neighbors and friends—and eventual relatives of a kind thanks to my parents being the first to marry within the families. They were also open-minded enough to be troubled by a particular strain of practice not uncommon within the Mennonite churches of the time. To their mind, many of the churches put forward the worst notion of the Protestant Reformation, which was the division between body and soul. This manifested itself in an adaptation of so-called self-denial. Grandpa Shudel put it this way. "They seem to forget Genesis says of this world, 'It is good. It is good. It is *very* good!'"

Soon after Grandma and Grandpa Shudel married, they approached their neighbors and friends, the Kiblers, about "planting a seed" for a new Mennonite church. The Shudels would deed a corner of their farm to the new church. They did not want to break away from the Swiss-German conference, the Old Mennonite Church; they had no interest in becoming a one-off non-denominational sect. "Church plants" such as this were common enough for the sheer practicality of them as large families grew by each generation. In their case, it had a bit less to do with natural growth in the township and more to do with the kind of growth they wanted their children to know as they grew up. Without getting into any real detail of the congregational polity they had in mind, the Shudels and Kiblers set off to get the blessing of both the congregation where they were members and the Old Mennonite Church. They were so respected that getting such an approval was perfunctory.

The polity they had in mind was simple enough. They would seek to maintain the parts they believed were the most faithful to the Gospel—living peaceably, simply and with humility and generosity. In all other aspects they would be— without knowing it at the time—progressive in terms of mental health and inclusion.

They could not reconcile in the Gospels, or in the world as they knew it in their lives as farmers, this division of body and soul; and they wanted their children to grow up in a support system that took the Old and New Testament directive to love God, yourself and your neighbor. It seemed to them that the Mennonites had adopted the love God and neighbor fairly well, but they made their individual salvation a worthiness test based on how sacrificial you could prove yourself to be. While a Mennonite might call this humility, it seemed to the Shudels and Kiblers this was just another veiled form of pride and not at all healthy. While many in the churches didn't live this way in reality, enough did to bother them —and way too often it was the message from the pulpit.

According to Grandma Shudel, all this did was "raise children who want to escape at the first opportunity."

Grandpa Kibler added, "You can't expect to make sense of your neighbor's world when you can't make sense of your own."

With their congregation and the Old Mennonite Church's blessing assured, they began meeting as a new church. One week would be on the Shudel farm and the next at the Kibler farm. While they knew and respected the Amish who never build a church building (and it must be said, saved a lot of money and upkeep in the process), they had every intention of building a church. Their reason was simple enough. According to my dad, Grandpa Kibler said, "You can't expect an outsider to feel welcome dropping in on some farm where they see a few cars or a couple of horse and buggies on a Sunday morning. You need a place where the door is open and the sign out front says, 'All are welcome.'"

With the Kibler mason skills and the Shudel carpentry skills, they set off to build a small church that would seat about a hundred people. This they thought was bigger than they needed by a long stretch, but when they were discussing it, the four church "planters" agreed on the process. They would sit quietly at the Shudel kitchen table in prayer. Each had a slip of paper and a pencil. When moved to do so, each would write a number on the paper for how many people the church should hold. They would then fold the paper and place it in the center of the table. Whatever all four slips totaled together would be divided by four and that would be the number.

Grandma Kibler was the designated tabulator for the results. She started to chuckle immediately. "You certainly made my adding and dividing easy," she said. All four had written the number 100. And so it was to be.

By sheer virtue of their skills, their little church would be more handsome than most Mennonite churches in the area. Grandpa Shudel found enough neighbors to help him build a timber, mortise and tenon frame. He always kept a stock of harvested poplar, pine, oak and hickory logs from his and other local farmers' woods for whatever barn, house or coop might need building. Grandpa Kibler bricked and rocked the entire exterior—random rubble rock that he gathered hither and yon from rocks taken out of fields in Michigan when farmers had begun to crop the land. The township's deep, rich topsoils had no native rock. The brick works in a nearby county made one color—red. Grandpa Kibler would have liked to have done the entire church in rock, but as he said to Grandpa Shudel, "If we ever have to build on, we might not find all the stone we need to blend in and may need to use mostly brick." He had a gift for "thinkin' down the road."

They stuck to the common practice of simple pews and clear glass windows—no stained glass in these churches and no instruments.

Grandpa Kibler seemed to be right about the difficulty with any church growth when you are meeting on a farm. Most weeks it was just the Shudels and Kiblers, and one other Shudel sibling and their family and one other Kibler sibling and their family. The new church plant, until the building was done, was strictly a family affair—and quite limited at that.

Enough from their old church and the township were curious that, for the dedication, the little church was packed to overflowing. Grandpa Shudel had carved these words over the front door:

Loving God
Loving Ourselves
Loving Others

To the Shudels and Kiblers, this represented the only creed they needed. They called their little congregation "Hope Mennonite" as they thought, after love, the greatest duty to their children was to instill a mind always towards hope. They felt that whatever noble intention the body-and-soul dividers had, they undermined hope with a despair that grew from the root of being so focused on their self-sacrificing. Again it must be said, they seem to have had an innate sense of good mental health too easily suppressed in many religious communities—not just the Mennonites.

It would be an entire generation before they ever would consider hiring a minister. As the church began to grow both through the family lines and curious neighbors who joined them, they cultivated their own "teachers"—as they would refer to the leadership taking turns on Sundays and Wednesday evenings leading the services.

Some churches still sat women and girls on one side and men and boys on the other. They considered retaining this practice for the practicality it provided them in singing their four-part harmony.

But Grandma Shudel scuttled the idea. She said, "The way the voices ring in this little church it will be just as worthy of the Lord if we sit as a family," adding, "and if those boys of ours wiggle around too much I can box their ears!"

Her children and grandchildren were greatly humored over the years by this, the most violent act in the family. Grandma Shudel would grab the ear of any of her kids and grandkids whenever she thought they needed to straighten up. In truth, it humored her in her old age as much as anyone as she'd recall this or that time one or the other of us "needed a good boxing."

I remember it well enough. I was a squirmer in the pew. We sat every Sunday right in front of her, and she seemed to know her best opportunity to box someone's ear was to be sure she was aligned directly behind me. I think she knew some Sundays my wiggling was as much to give her the opportunity as it was my inherent restless self. She would be the grandma I knew the best and longest. I adored her! She died when I was in eighth grade.

The Kibler farm was just south of the Shudel farm and they shared a common property line. The Kiblers deeded to the church enough land out of the north corner of their farm for a graveyard. And so it was that all my grandparents would be buried in Hope Cemetery as would my own parents when their time came.

Chapter Six

It sometimes happens in "church plants" where, over time, the original intent ends up morphing into the opposite of the founders. Often a church starts when they think their group has gotten too "liberal" or too "conservative," and over time they become the liberals or conservatives the founders thought they were leaving behind. At least through my upbringing, Hope Mennonite was not one of those churches. I've always speculated that was mostly due to their polity of having their own internally nurtured teachers who stuck to the basics as first envisioned. While this can lead to the inbreeding of narrow ideologies, their humility to the Gospel seemed to keep any tendencies in this direction well at bay.

With the families from my grandparents on both sides and the siblings' families from each side, within ten years there were thirty-two regulars just from the Shudel and Kibler families. As soon as they opened their doors, the Mennonite family who lived directly across the road from Grandma and Grandpa Kibler, the Grabers, started coming to Hope. They also had some Lutheran neighbors, but none of them were adventurous enough to see if they might like Hope. Still, enough from around the township came to where there were a faithful eighty-some in membership. The "some," of course, varied according to births and deaths, but the core of families attending was consistent. No one, even up to my time there, ever left in a huff. They seemed to know they had a good thing and cherished and nurtured it with genuine gratitude for it.

By the time the children of these families started to approach adulthood, Grandpa Shudel thought he might need to deed more land to the church, but he needed enough acreage to keep his stock. When he had the opportunity to buy eighty acres that backed up to his east property line, he snatched it up which gave him another 40 acres of tillable land and 40 more acres of woods with a good mix of oak, hickory and hard maple. His woods on the old homeplace lacked much in the way of hard maple, having been lost to a good many beautiful maple cabinets and tables—and he was glad to finally have some trees to tap for maple syrup.

The Kiblers, Schudels and Grabers were always keeping a keen eye out for any farms within the township that might come up for sale so they could begin to help their kids set up their own farmsteads. I never understood completely how they managed to pull it off. Certainly, none of the families were from wealthy backgrounds, but between the modest price of land back in those days and their frugality they managed to buy 80-acre tracts for each of their kids—boy or girl. Another trait of those Hope Mennonites was their very egalitarian ethos which was not portioned out to one gender in favor of the other.

These farms were not deeded as gifts, but rather a way for them to start on their own. Each son or daughter was expected to pay one-thirtieth of the purchase price of the farm every January 1st. They charged no interest. They didn't even place a lien on the properties. It would have been easy enough for one to sell off their farm and abscond with the proceeds. None did. If both matriarch and patriarch died before the thirty years when the farm would be "paid in full," it was the understanding by all that the residual loan balance would be calculated into any inheritance due so that all came out as even as possible in the end. As best I could tell, their egalitarianism was as Swiss as it was Mennonite— and being both made them solid as a rock in this regard.

The Hope church founders had designed their little brick-and-rock, timber frame almost square—in fact, except for the little foyer at the entrance, the sanctuary was wider than it was long. They wanted it wide enough to be able to easily build out the east end when and if an expansion was needed so that the addition, as Grandpa Shudel would put it, "wouldn't look like a sore thumb." When the time did come they decided some simple math was easy enough to figure how big they ought to make any additions. They could see the families coming on, and except for one of the thirteen children between them, none appeared to be making any plans for leaving the township or the church.

This time around, they had all the labor they needed just from the membership. Still, a couple of their Lutheran neighbors offered to help as well. They more than doubled the length of the sanctuary, added a large transept to the north side near the front and connected a large fellowship hall, kitchen, bathrooms (which up until then were outhouses), and a nursery-playroom. Now they could seat 300. Grandma Kibler said, "This a good number from our original one hundred—now we've got a hundred each for Father, Son, and Holy Ghost." This was as big as each of them thought a church should be, making it pretty well established as unwritten doctrine that after that, some families needed to go off and start a new church plant if the church became too big to accommodate the new growth. That was not a problem they would face in my grandparents' day, but it was one Hope Mennonite would have to reckon with one day—and the founders would have been greatly disappointed in the result.

Chapter Seven

By the time I came along, my Grandpa Kibler was dead, Grandpa Shudel died on my sixth birthday, and Grandma Kibler in the middle of a blizzard on Christmas one year later. Of my twelve aunts and uncles on both sides, except for one uncle and his family, all were Hope Mennonite members.

The eldest Kibler son, Uncle Christian, was killed in an auto accident soon after he was married so my in-law aunt, Ilah, ended up leaving their farm and moving back into town. Ilah was an only child, and both her parents had died in a car crash as well when she was a senior in high school. Grief just seemed to pile up on her, but it could never extinguish her kind and generous spirit.

Not surprisingly, my Grandma and Grandpa Shudel insisted she keep the proceeds from the sale of the farm to help provide for herself. They realized she might remarry and not need the extra money, but they also figured it was theirs to give away if they wanted to and so they did. As it turned out, she kept coming to Hope Mennonite and never did remarry.

Aunt Ilah got a job as a teller in the bank and certainly gave back generously to the Mennonite Disaster Fund and the Mennonite Central Committee which Hope Mennonite supported. Of all the aunts, she did anything and everything she could for her nieces and nephews. She never forgot a birthday, never found an excuse not to babysit, and managed to give every graduating senior a nice card with a generous check enclosed. She was amazing. In town she kept a backyard full of raspberry bushes—no other garden—and as the annual harvest would come in, she would be dropping off quarts of raspberries to all the siblings' farms.

Once I asked her why she didn't have any strawberries.

She said, "I don't like bending over that much having to pick 'em. And like unto it, I don't have any fruit trees because I never liked working with anything over my head—pickin' fruit or changin' a light fixture."

I loved going to her house, which we did on a weekly basis in the spring and summer. As we grew up, we were her dedicated lawn mowers—as soon as we could push a mower. She never had a riding mower—didn't even have a mower with a motor! She had one of those old reel mowers that worked you silly and which forced you to mow as quick as the grass grew. Some weeks that meant two mowings. She sharpened it herself and made sure it was never dull for our hard work.

Inside she was an immaculate housekeeper (while our house was sometimes a little scattered from kids who knew how to make a mess more than how to tidy-up), and she had a gigantic fern in each of her two big windows in the dining room. She kept big sets of Lincoln Logs and Legos which she would haul out every time she babysat me, and she'd get on the floor with me to build something. And we didn't stack things up willy-nilly. She would be sure I interlocked things as one would do building a building to ensure it was done properly. For some of my cousins, who were a lot more book-oriented than I was at that age, she kept a collection of every classic book imaginable for early to advanced readers. I have no idea if she ever read or not. I never saw her read, but she might well have been an avid reader when the mayhem of other people's children was at bay.

Aunt Ilah's ancestors were mostly French. Whether that's the reason I'm not sure, but she was much more of a hugger than we firm Swiss stock. I was also the only niece or nephew she could never hug unless I was at her house. Whenever she came to our house, my dog, Spicer, would get between me and Aunt Ilah as soon as she entered. Spicer would never bite her, but she would stand there barking at her—not giving an inch. Aunt Ilah would say to her, "What did I ever do to you?" As funny as that was to watch, I was humored even more when years later I reconnected the events of Aunt Ilah's death and Spicer's death. Spicer died just a couple of days after she had died—and I guess went to bark at her in the hereafter—or to get there in plenty of time in case I showed up unexpectedly.

Aunt Ilah always seemed the picture of health, but in her fifties she just dropped over dead. We were all so shocked. Unbeknownst to me, she had left with her will some instructions for her service which asked that I sing at her funeral. She didn't say what I should sing, and I didn't really know what her favorite song might be. A survey of family didn't yield any help on that score. I settled on *Great is Thy Faithfulness* because it seemed to me for someone who married into the family, none were as faithful to the family as she. While the song is about the faithfulness of God to us, it seemed to me her godliness was every bit as faithful to us kids.

Chapter Eight

I'm not sure how they worked it out exactly, but as long as I can remember it was established that the Kiblers would get together as a family every Thanksgiving and the Shudels every Christmas. There was no leaving one to go to the other on any one holiday. It appeared to me from my cousins that they mostly stuck to this in each of their families as well. I'm not sure how they juggled the in-law side though I do know that some just weren't as close as the Kiblers and Shudels and probably weren't that keen on spending the holidays together. Too many were from that old "divided-body-and-soul" crowd who took themselves a bit too seriously. And as my Grandma Shudel had predicted, many left the church and the area at the first opportunity. We were all soldered in place at Hope Mennonite— soldered—that's not the right word. We were rooted there in all the best sense of the word.

My other aunts and uncles all farmed, of course, with the Shudel men working as well as carpenters when the farm didn't demand as much of their labor (and it must be said as their growing children could assume more chores), while the Kibler men learned the mason trade. My dad was more farmer than mason, though he would help out if push came to shove. He liked all things mechanical, so he was more inclined to work on the tractors of both sides of the family and also maintained some of the shared machinery that each side of the family owned like the combines and balers. It was almost a matter of course by the time I came along that the kids were doing the bulk of the farming for the uncles, while they were making a living off the farm, building many fine brick homes around the township—and even the wider county. They were so busy in the summers that by my time, I worked every summer helping out. They would split me up—one summer tending mason and one on the carpenter crew. While I preferred sawdust over mortar, I preferred both over the grease and oil my dad seemed to like best.

Like every Mennonite family I've ever known, the aunts and my mother had gardens the size of a football field (or so it seemed) and canned like mad come summertime. What we didn't grow they bought in bulk and froze or canned. These were mostly cherries from Wisconsin and blueberries from Michigan. Apples, pears, peaches and apricots were plentiful in all our orchards—especially peach trees. The only nuts we ever had were walnuts from a few huge trees that were out by the road and seemed to faithfully produce an all-you-could-eat, all-year supply—if you were willing to crack 'em.

As I learned at my Grandma Kibler's funeral, she took the canning madness to a whole different level. Each year the Mennonites would collect food for children's homes. Most people contributed a few jars and called it good enough. Grandma Kibler and her girls literally filled up the entire back end of a pickup— with side boards—so that the cases of canned fruits, vegetables, mincemeat, pumpkin and soups (chicken and beef) were stacked up nearly four feet high. As you can imagine, not only was it quite a production, the girls who thought she was half crazy when they were doing it every year would carry those canning days as the greatest memory of her, and always recall it with laughter and tears.

"Progress" being what it is, home-canned goods fell out of the acceptable donation strategy by my time, so those poor children's homes were certainly downgraded in my mind "for food safety's sake" from Grandma Kibler's perfected canning to Del Monte, Dole and Campbells. The corporation always seems to win in the end.

Chapter Nine

Mom and Dad agreed that Grandpa Kibler was the best singer in the family. He knew a number of the old German chants and would often sing them as he worked in the barn or laid stone. He had a strong baritone voice and would sit in a rocker in his old age, singing his favorite songs he'd learned after coming to America. His two favorites were *Abide with Me* and *Amazing Grace*. Whenever the entire family was gathered, he would always conclude the gathering leading, *God Be With You Till We Meet Again*.

God be with you till we meet again;
By his counsels guide, uphold you;
With his sheep securely fold you.
God be with you till we meet again.

Till we meet, till we meet,
Till we meet at Jesus' feet,
Till we meet, till we meet,
God be with you till we meet again.

God be with you till we meet again;
When life's perils thick confound you,
Put his arms unfailing round you.
God be with you till we meet again.

Till we meet, till we meet,
Till we meet at Jesus' feet,
Till we meet, till we meet,
God be with you till we meet again.

When Mom and Dad dropped me off at college, Dad thought I should sing Grandpa's departing song. He recalled how beautifully Grandpa sang it.

I said to Dad, "I guess you're admitting that Grandpa liked to sing and had a better solo voice than I have."

He said, "All I'll admit is, he did a lot less fussin' about it. He did have a rich voice that stood out. It could be that richness was tied to his age, and you might grow into his voice one day if you keep at it. I'm afraid I got the Leichti voice from your grandma, but you're a Kibler. Could be your grandchildren will remember you sitting in the rocking chair as an old man singing them inspiring hymns."

I said, "Could be I won't have any grandchildren, but if I ever do, I'll remember you imagined me keeping the Kibler legacy alive."

To that he said, "I don't know whose going to take care of you in your old age if you don't have any grandchildren."

I thought of a good comeback to that, saying, "There's no proof at this point your grandchildren are going to take care of you. Could be, you'll be surprised how quickly they put you in a home."

To that he said, "Humility would require me to acknowledge that may well be true—not very comforting. If you don't have children, I'll just come live with you."

Mom had been silent till now, "August, that ought to be motivation for you to get married and have a passel of children. Not everyone has my gift of patience."

Dad said, "As usual, I get you two ganging up to pick on me."

We just chuckled. We never did get around to singing Grandpa Kibler's parting song. We all forgot that's what started it all.

I remember Grandma Kibler would softly sing that song in German when she was working in the kitchen. I even remember it when I'd stand on a kitchen chair watching her cut up chickens at the sink. She'd be singing as she worked, *Gott mit euch, bis wir uns wiedersehen*, and then she'd put her hand up in the chicken to push against the lungs and get one last squawk out of the headless bird. Of course, this was for my benefit and surprised the living daylights out of me the first time she ever did it. After that I'd say, "Make it squawk, Grandma." She'd make it squawk and carry right on with her singing.

When I was in eighth grade, Hope Mennonite took its next big leap into the modern age. Actually it took two leaps. The first was to buy a grand piano for the sanctuary which marked the first instrument to be used in the church services. That was easy enough to ease into as they still sang four-part a cappella but enjoyed the preludes, postludes and offertories my gifted cousin, Janet, would play.

The other "modernization" was anything but benign and not a bit beneficial. The council felt like the church had grown to the point that a full-time minister should be hired. The long-standing tradition of internal leadership would be retired so far as the Sunday pulpit duties were required. Hope was one of the last hold-outs on this score. It was the only Mennonite church around without a full-time or at least part-time minister—and had been for many years. They were eager to give a young man an early opportunity—I'd be out of college before Mennonites would be ordaining any women.

My Uncle Hans, Mom's oldest brother, was head of the search committee and contacted the seminary in Elkhart to let them know the church was interested in calling a recent graduate as their first pastor. The posting was put up at the seminary and one young man quickly applied. He had a very positive letter of recommendation from the dean, and they proceeded with interviewing the man and letting him preach in the pulpit one Sunday. As no other graduates had "put their name in the hopper" as Uncle Hans would put it, the church held a vote and the call was extended.

Now instead of "Brother Kibler" or "Sister Graber" leading the service, it would be Rev. Nutt—the same reverend who insisted my soul was in peril for not knowing the "day and hour."

All I knew at the time was he didn't stay around long—long enough to cause me my first challenge to dogma that my mind would deal with as a lifelong doubter of other's certainty. It was only when Mom shared her deeper truth of my precarious birth that I learned the rest of the story.

Rev. Nutt's bachelor's degree was from a "conservative" Christian university. I really detest the co-opting of that term "conservative." There is really nothing conservative about most people (at least in my adult life span) who proudly clutch that label for themselves. The core curriculum at these "conservative" schools is jingoism and adherence to Biblical inerrancy from the 100 level to the 400 level—four years of indoctrination. They wrap themselves in the flag, supporting the militarization and hardline tactics of the law-and-order, American-exceptionalism war hawks. Then they layer on top of that the Bible which they have turned into an idol—as they use it to thump everyone over the head with their dogmatic interpretations. Finally, because Jesus is coming back soon to take them to heaven, the related word to their label of choice, "conservation," is a throw-away word for the "progressives"—as the earth was given to man to dominate and by god there is no way we can run out of fresh air, clean water, or rich soil before God "calls us home." But I'm wandering off point.

The Rev. Nutt somehow ended up at the Mennonite seminary for reasons no one fully understood. He wasn't at Hope Mennonite three months before more were unhappy with his clear view to dogma over grace, and so it was decided Uncle Hans would make an appointment with the dean who had written the glowing letter and drive to Elkhart to talk with him.

Uncle Hans started out, "Something hasn't seemed to take with that young man during his time here. I'd expect his kind of preaching in the denomination he grew up in, but we thought he'd left that behind. Now we are all supposed to be 'warriors for Christ' and get out there and beat the bushes to make sure those 'sinners' around us know we are 'the chosen.' It would seem all Catholics are going to hell and Lutherans aren't far behind. It isn't sitting at all well with peaceable folk. More are going home mad than fed."

The dean responded, "Mr. Shudel, you laid out the problem concisely, and I can certainly see there is a serious problem. If you read my letter of recommendation again, you would see that I extolled his academic achievements which were real and I 'believed' he had potential as a pastor to his people. Measuring academic achievement is easy. Measuring their pastoral abilities is a lot harder.

"When the men are here, they are under authority and they want to make a good impression. Most fall into this category. A few follow more along the non-conformist route even in seminary, and I can pretty well see they are going to favor the more prophetic role in the church. They often end up in active global service through the Mennonite Central Committee trying to do meaningful work helping the impoverished and in peace and justice initiatives.

There are men who have both pastoral and prophetic gifts, but these are more the exception than the rule." Smiling he added, "Most of the men we see come through here will be good pastors and not overly prophetic!

"Your reverend, as you have described him, seems to be one of those fellows who forgets their submission to authority doesn't end when they graduate. It merely transfers to the congregation they are called to serve. Unfortunately, there are those who very quickly think they *are* the authority and the congregants theirs to mold to *their* likeness. That certainly sounds like the problem here.

"I'll tell you what I'll do. I'll drive over and have a long talk with him. If it seems like he's willing to face up to his hard-line approach and try another way, I will let you know, and hopefully you will see quick improvement. If it doesn't seem like there is hope for that, then I'll suggest he look into employment in his old denomination—that the Mennonites probably aren't ever going to be the fit he is looking for."

Uncle Hans said to him, "Everything you said makes sense of our bewilderment about the situation. We very much appreciate your help and guidance through all this. We're glad to be patient with him if he's willing to work with us instead of against us."

The two prayed together, and Uncle Hans returned and called each member of the council to update them. A couple of days later, Dad saw a car pull into the church mid-morning and saw a man get out in a suit—he figured it was the dean. His car was there a long time. Hope Mennonite would never know all that was discussed that day, but the next Sunday Rev. Nutt asked for a meeting of the church council after the service. There, he announced his intention to seek a calling in his former denomination and hoped he could stay on until he found something—provided it didn't take longer than a few months at which point he would leave whether "called to a pulpit" or not. While none of the group were too eager for three more months of being warriors for Christ, it seemed the generous thing to do, and Hope was always generous. Fortunately, he found "a calling" near the end of the second month, and in the meantime, he stuck to benign-enough sermons to keep the peaceable lot from leaving mad if not fed.

It would be almost two years before they tried hiring another full-time minister. They reverted to their shared-leadership model and as Mom put it (who was still on council during all this), "The next time we knew to pay more attention to the Spirit and less to the transcripts and letters of recommendation."

Chapter Ten

There are good neighbors and then there are good neighbors. Our Lutheran neighbors were good neighbors. We knew their kids in the small township school we attended and would attend a wedding or funeral as such came along, just as they would attend our family weddings and funerals. Beyond that, all we could lay claim to was saying we were neighbors. There wasn't any borrowing a cup of sugar or getting together for anything but larger community events. There was no sharing of time to babysit or give someone a ride into town. If something broke down or, as was more frequent, got stuck in the field, they weren't solicited for help. As far as I ever knew, there weren't any common relatives in the ancestry between us. Where their families emigrated from was just assumed to be Germany, which it probably was—though as mentioned before, there were some Kiblers who passed along this erroneous notion as well.

Then there are neighbors! Directly across our township gravel road were the Grabers. The generation who lived there in my time was the same generation as my parents. It was the "old Graber homeplace," and the only son, Conrad Graber, moved his wife, Marie, and their young family in when his parents "retired to town." Like my folks, they had four children. We were boy-girl-girl-boy. Their kids were each a year older and were boy-girl-boy-girl. One would think that as close as we were as neighbors, at least one of us from each family would have followed in the Kibler-Shudel tradition and married. None did. We were distant relatives, but not close enough to keep that from being the issue. Their great-grandmother and our great-grandfather were brother and sister. It was our common great-great-grandmother who was drug from the house to translate for the Germans. We didn't know any of that as kids. We were just neighbors.

I don't know if all children attach to certain adults in their world beyond their own family, but I can say unequivocally, I adored Conrad and Marie. Perhaps, I need to elaborate on the word adore just a bit. I'm sure they must have had their grumpy days. I certainly did. My parents did. My siblings were either grumpy or causing me to be so—Wayne almost every day and my sisters at

36

least every other day! Yet, I can't recall a single time ever where I would walk into their house or barn or wherever they were that they didn't look directly at me with bright eyes and smiles, making a small boy feel like he was important to them. That probably sounds silly to some, but even as the years advance and I look back on their faces in my memory, I still feel the warmth and joy their lives seemed to exude with no effort.

Conrad was Hope Mennonite in a nutshell—humble, loving and generous. He never worked off the farm—at least that I ever knew. He would do many things the old way. That is to say, breed his own stock, milk a few cows by hand for their milk, cheese and butter, butcher his own hogs and smoke the hams, always keeping some land in pasture for his cattle. He also kept a dog or two on the farm, and when he was going to the mill he would sometimes take me along. We never had a dog on the farm until he took care of that. Before my earliest memories, my mom said Conrad came across the road one day carrying a little, newly weaned puppy from a litter of his one female dog. "August should have a dog," was all he said and handed the puppy to the little boy sitting on the floor nearby. Thus began my love of dogs. Mom named her Spicer.

Conrad liked to sit in the woods. During deer-hunting season he would take a rifle with him as though he was going to hunt. He would always come back empty-handed. We all knew it had nothing to do with a scarcity of deer and everything to do with not being able to kill one when he saw it.

Marie and my mother were best friends. Neither was inclined to drive tractor in the spring like some farm wives would or take on milking the cows, but they both were incredibly hard workers. There was no lack of eggs or chicken meat for all the layers and broilers they each raised. They both could bake up a storm. When Marie would make her huge homemade glazed yeast donuts, we'd be invited over while they were still warm. My mom made her famous cinnamon rolls with equal generosity to these neighbors across the road. There was a regular traipsing of one child or the other across the road to get whatever provision had come up short for what was going on in the kitchen. There was no habit of running to town every time some little thing like a cup of sugar, flour or lard was needed—not when it was in stock across the road.

Marie had the best laugh ever. We all just loved to hear her get tickled by one thing or another. She had a brother who was a real character so when he was around, it was particularly fun to watch. She would cackle at everything he would say.

One Sunday evening when I was probably nine or ten, after we'd finished supper I went outside and strolled over to their house. As was the custom, I went to the back door which went straight into their kitchen. They were just sitting down for their Sunday supper. I don't know what I had in mind with my visit. I just recall sitting there like I belonged. And they seemed to include me just as naturally—at least it seemed to me that way at the time. After a while the phone rang. Marie answered. I didn't know who it was, but I heard her part of the conversation.

"Yes, he's here in the kitchen with us. Okay, I'll send him home."

My mother apparently had figured out all four were accounted for save one—and got to wondering where I'd gone since my bike was in the backyard, and I was nowhere else to be found.

After hanging up, Marie said, "That was your mom. She was looking for you and said to come home."

I didn't get any chastisement for my unannounced adventure— at least none I recall—though I guess the search call did keep me from ever doing it again.

Wayne was over helping with the chores once when Conrad had broken his leg falling off the tractor. I'm not sure where the Graber boys were—I suspect Dad sent Wayne over to be neighborly. I doubt very much Wayne would have done it of his own accord. I do know the girls were up in the straw mow pitching down bales for Wayne to spread out in the barn. Just as he came back for the next bale, instead of a bale down came Grace, the youngest. She was the size of a toothpick and wiry. Maybe her lack of gravitational mass helped, but she laid there for a second looking up at Wayne who was still adjusting to the "bale" that had come down from the mow before he said, "You all right?" She just giggled and got up, returning to the mow to carry on.

Unlike the family get-togethers, we never had big meals together or barbecued together or anything like that with the Grabers. But we had plenty of interactions. Of course, we had church and school in common but also 4-H where both boys and girls took a steer to the county fair every year. The boys often entered corn or chickens as well and the girls always sewed something for display at the fair. In the winter our dads would pull us behind a tractor on sleds and toboggans and when the ditch or some flooded patch in a field would freeze, we kids would ice skate on it.

There was one other tradition between our families which was a full-family affair. Every New Year's Eve, our families would gather in the early evening and spend the next hours together to ring in the new year. One year would be at their house and the next at ours. Sometimes it wouldn't be too cold out and we kids would go in the yard and either play hide-and-seek or pitch a kickball over the house in some game that had some point which I can no longer recall. It involved hollering something as you did so but again, memory fails. I hope we did this anyway. If I've created this out of the ether, I may not be as sound of mind as I credit myself as being.

The night would always include party mix, cheese and crackers, sugar cookies, sandwiches—all fun food that could sit around all night. It seemed to me the girls were always the most enthusiastic when it came time for the final countdown—*TEN, NINE, EIGHT, SEVEN, SIX, FIVE, FOUR, THREE, TWO, ONE—HAPPY NEW YEAR!*

No kazoos! I never saw one of those until my college days. Perhaps it was the Mennonite propensity against instruments. There was no TV on all evening. This was just the township-road-countdown based on whatever clock was handy.

Even though we had our yearly family gatherings at Thanksgiving and Christmas, to this day nothing brings back the memories of the "celebration of the season" like the New Year's Eve gathering of our two families. I know this is just as true for the Graber kids as it is for me—as the two nearest my age have confirmed it.

There was one New Year's that held its own special memories. It was a night of blizzardy, below-zero cold. Our usual already-cold, drafty farmhouse didn't stand a chance trying to keep warm. The furnace ran nonstop. We had covers hanging over the drapes over the north-side and west-side windows, and everyone sat on the old huge radiators that were the only sources of heat. We were in coats, gloves and stocking hats. Still, we managed to eat homemade ice cream while sitting on the radiators!

Which reminds me—I slept in the coldest room in the house. It was on nights like this my sweet siblings would holler out to one of the others not yet in bed, "Shut August's door! It's making the whole upstairs cold!"

Marching Off to War

Chapter Eleven

None of my grandfathers or great-grandfathers or great-great grandfathers (as far as I know) ever shot anyone or served in a military role that might require them to do so. Mennonites, like the Brethren and Quakers, were conscientious objectors (COs) and would not do a few basic things assumed as normal for a citizen of the United States. They did not vote, fly a flag, serve in a combatant position in the armed services or own a handgun. (I did for a time vote and flew a flag, though I never served in a combatant position or owned a gun.) It is impossible to live in this country (and most countries for that matter) where the pressure to conform to a certain brand of nationalism to define one's patriotism isn't pretty intense. In times of war, it really ratchets up.

The Kiblers and Shudels were so intertwined as a family, when World War II came along the boys on both sides of the family began to question their Mennonite pacifism. The body-and-soul-divider Mennonites made it pretty clear that to do so meant leaving the church—shunned as it were or excommunicated as it might be more widely understood. While the Hope Mennonite founders could have never gone to war, they found their boys pushing the notion that they thought they should enlist. This was not a universal notion, but boys on each side of the family were thinking about it.

Four went to Europe and four came home—in and of itself, rather remarkable. Dad's oldest brother, Christian, and Mom's brothers Hans and Peter would be in active service. Her brother Mike was a non-combatant. All four were scattered around France and Belgium. The last thing Grandpa Shudel said to his three boys as they left was, "You know you don't have to do this." Beyond that, he let them make their own decision and their own way as he always did. What their return would mean for Hope Mennonite remained to be seen. They would not be shunned or excommunicated. The group was far too egalitarian and inclusive to even contemplate doing so, though the larger church would have perhaps pushed for it if they had been more on the radar within the denomination.   The boys were part of the church and the community. They couldn't conceive of casting them out for any reason.

But war changes people—and sometimes when alienation and separation happen it is rather self-inflicted. This happened with Peter on his return. He grew to resent those at Hope who hadn't gone to war and assumed that unfortunate pride that seems to come, more than not, with having served. He started taking his family to a non-denominational, evangelical church.   While this grieved both families, they did not try to intervene on his decision to leave Hope.

My dad's brother Christian went to war and Dad did not. Fortunately, they seemed to pick up where they left off before the war. In truth, one of them needed to stay home and farm and Dad, being the more inclined to full-time farming stayed on the farm where he would later raise his own family. Being the youngest, this may have been Grandpa Kibler's plan all along as he was one farm short of buying a farm for each child—leaving the homeplace for the last.   Dad, instead of registering as a conscientious objector applied for an agriculture deferment and it was granted.

His school chum, Conrad, who would take over the Graber homestead after WWII, spent his service during the war working in a mental hospital. I've wondered, but never thought to ask, if this was a hospital for soldiers driven mad by war.   Like Uncle Mike, Conrad's brothers were noncombatants in the military—working with the medics on the front line. Uncle Mike served as a stretcher bearer—a job his combat-serving brothers did not envy.   They appreciated anyone who could deal with the blood, guts and death those poor men had to deal with day in and day out. He certainly came out with the firmest resolve of all, taking a stand against the futility of war. He would move heaven and earth before he let any of his boys go to Vietnam when that mess appeared on the scene.

I never heard any of the Grabers talk about their dad's time at the mental hospital, but I have to think during his tenure, surely those poor patients had to know the compassion and dignity that his gentle soul was sure to offer them. If he ever looked with even a hint of condescension on another human being, I never spotted it.

Across the road at our farm, there was plenty of eye-rolling toward a good many neighbors and relatives for one reason or another.

By the time Vietnam rolled around only my oldest brother, Wayne, had the luck of the draw of having to decide whether to let the military scoop him up or register as a CO. I think the peer pressure from the mostly non-Mennonite crowd he seemed to run with in high school pushed him into signing up. Flunking out of college his first semester didn't help. He went over, and he came back home. The trip home was in a box covered with a flag. He'd gone down with three others when the helicopter they were in was shot down. Fortunately, he hadn't married before going, but that was little comfort to peaceable parents grieving their eldest son.

His legacy consists of a small plaque the town put in the smaller of its two parks. I never knew either Mom or Dad to ever go see it —including when the city placed it there. We kids went—they did not. I suppose to them the plaque was little more than another form of idolatry which Mennonites and other Anabaptists were firmly against—thus their stance against flag flying, statues, and even figures in stained glass windows. I would find myself moving closer to this as my own article of faith as the years progressed. Maybe by the time I'm old and decrepit, I'll have any and all such idols as may remain out of my life. Long before I was old and decrepit, I certainly embraced the peaceable way of my ancestors and would always be firmly against my country's wars.

One thing Mom and Dad did do every year was take flowers to Wayne's grave on Decoration Day. I know they kept the flag the government had sent with the coffin, but I never knew it or any other to fly on our farm.

Certainly, the impact of war wouldn't bear down on our family in the same way as it might have if Wayne had been married and had children. My uncles who went as combatants and noncombatants all came back home intact—at least physically. I'm sure they must have carried emotional scars they never talked about and took those secrets with them to their grave.

Miles and I came along at a time when President Ford not only eliminated the draft, he even eliminated the need to register. That didn't last long. The next president would reinstate draft

43

registration when one turned eighteen, but still Miles and I never had to register.

I was raised with enough charity of spirit not to ever want to condemn any who serve. Getting help with a college or home loan after they have served seems like some necessary compensation— but the better way to honor them would be to not send them off on fool's errand for the rich and powerful. A hope that remains but not yet realized so far in my lifetime.

Miles' dad was in the army at the start of the "Korean conflict," which he would never talk about. Then he had a very short stint as a military contractor—doing exactly what, he never would say. He came back ill, dehydrated and forever jaded. That was in Vietnam, and all he would say to Miles was, "If this country knew what their government was really doing, people would blow their brains out."

School Days

Chapter Twelve

I blame a lot of my disdain for "school" on school consolidation. I would feel the force of it in the sixth grade. For my first several years of school we all (the Kibler and Shudel cousins and the Grabers) attended our little township school which ran through eighth grade. For high school you had to pick one of the nearby town schools in other townships, but for those first eight years (they didn't have kindergarten until I was in first grade) all kids in the township attended the township school. There was actually no town in our township unless you counted that one school building, the township trustee building and garage and a general store, that was part grocery store, hardware store and gas station. We were farm families and a few families living on farmsteads with rented land, where one or both parents drove into one of the nearby towns to work at a mill or factory or some store.

The best part of that school was everyone in the class was friends with everyone else. It didn't matter what church you went to or whether you were from a well-to-do family or one struggling to get by. About a quarter of my classmates were "Mexican" kids whose families had settled permanently when their parents got jobs in the local factories or about town. They were a mix of Catholics and converts to the Mennonite faith. In fact, they built their own Mennonite church, and it was equal in size to the expanded Hope Mennonite. Most had come up from Texas as migrant laborers somewhere in their past and just stayed. I think the majority of the families were originally from Mexico, but the label perhaps was more the generic immigrant term of the time rather than actual fact. (We weren't enlightened to the terms hispanic or latino(a) in those days.) They were every bit a part of our close-knit world.

No place is perfect, nor any one class. Our class had one misfit, bad-Billy, who was as ornery as they come and wanted so much to be a bully. We never called him bad-Billy to his face, but certainly thought about doing so. We kept that one notch above his level on the hope he might soften someday. Given the closeness of all the rest of us, bad-Billy had no real power over any of us to bully anyone. If he did try to pick on any boy or girl, one or more of us were there to fend him off. Our poor fifth grade teacher got the worst of it. Billy would sass back to her at any opportunity. She liked our class—except for him—and had moved with us from fourth to fifth grade. I'd wondered if she'd move with us to sixth. One day he stood right in front of her at the front of the class mouthing off about something—I don't remember what. It was her reaction that stuck in my mind.

She momentarily lost control of her usual composure and slapped him right across the face. I don't think it fazed him—he was probably too used to it from home. But I remember her reaction. She immediately put both hands up to her face and began to cry—her head and shoulders shaking in the fear, shame and frustration that had brought her to that one momentary loss of control. I don't know whether the principal was ever made aware, nor am I sure that if he was he would have done much about it. He'd certainly used the paddle on bad-Billy plenty of times, as such was normal recourse for the unruly in those days. I saw the paddle in the principal's office but never had the misfortune of having it applied to my backside. And I don't recall anyone else in our class ever getting sent to the principal's office for disciplinary reasons. The worst we ever got was two minutes standing in the corner.

I did tell Mom and Dad about the events of the day and Dad said, "The poor boy gets it honestly. His dad thinks his shit don't stink and he'd lie even if the truth sounded better."

All I knew about their family was that the mother, Rose, was my mother's second cousin some way or the other. Rose went to a little Brethren church but her husband never did, and he was only too glad for "his boys" to be manly and stay home on Sundays as well. Poor Rose only had boys—five of them. My mom knew the old cuss would only dole out money to Rose if he had to, as though her labor on the farm was something owed to him. Rose was a sweet woman and Mom felt so sorry for her. Mom would make about any excuse to drop by and visit for a few minutes, and she would always take something with her—a flat of eggs, a couple jars of mincemeat, tomatoes from the garden. She always tried to go on the day she thought the old cuss would be in town at the mill.

Later that same school year, Mom stopped by, and his pickup was there. When she went to the kitchen door to knock, she could see through the half-glass door the old cuss standing at the kitchen counter picking at a ham. Rose was out of sight, but must have been just standing at the stove. I overheard Mom recounting all this to Dad that evening. I'm sure Mom didn't realize I was within earshot.

She said, "I almost turned around, but he saw me so I knocked, and he said to Rose and clearly loud enough he wanted me to hear, 'I wish you'd tell that old Kibler bitch to quit coming around here.' The only reason he even said it was to humiliate her. He knew it wouldn't frighten me away. If you could have seen the look on Rose's face when she came to the door! All I could do was shake my head, and all she could do was fight back tears."

That was the one and only time I ever heard my mother say anything that could be classified as vulgar language. Of course, she was just quoting the old cuss—and she was certainly anything but an old Kibler bitch. I suppose someone who didn't possess my mother's fortitude might have walked away crying and never gone back. She'd be back two weeks later with a few jars of her delicious canned peaches for Rose.

As our little church grew, there were no divorces in the families until I was already gone to college. Whether there should have been or not is another matter. After Mom's encounter with the old cuss, one night at the dinner table after her latest trip to Rose's, she said something that surprised all us kids—probably Dad, too.

She laid out her mind on the matter. "Some women get mixed up with a man who is nothing but trouble. My poor cousin, Rose, who certainly doesn't deserve it, puts up with that cruel man in her house—he keeps it from being a real home. I wish she'd take the kids and leave. I don't see a point in calling anything a marriage if the vows of one of them mean nothing."

She finished saying, "Her preacher is always telling the congregation to honor their husbands. A man has to have honor to even be a husband, and that old cuss of Rose's has no honor. If I ever hear Hope Mennonite preach such nonsense I'm going to stand up and set the preacher straight on the matter."

Chapter Thirteen

There was one other boy in our class from a "troubled home" but none of us knew it at the time. He was my best pal, though he was also the shyest and most withdrawn kid in the class. We would walk up and down the hall of the school with our arms around each other's shoulder and always try to get on the same team for kickball or softball. His name was Wesley, and he was one of those kinda goofy-looking kids whose ears grew faster than the rest of him. He had sandy-colored hair which was kept longer than most of the boys'. He had big round eyes and a small frame. He got better looking as he grew into those ears, and while I never saw him after high school, I've always thought his baby face probably afforded him the good looks and young appearance we gray and wrinkled lot envy.

The only thing that marred that baby face was a small scar over his eye and a couple others on his chin. He also had a few on his arms and other places generally hidden out of view—some perhaps hidden by his hair. It seemed he was accident-prone when he was at home on the farm, or at least that's the story he told. We should have had the sense to put two and two together as I never once saw him injure himself at school. We were far less clued into the reality of what some children endure at home in those days. Besides, they were a "good Mennonite family."

At the end of our school year in fifth grade my cousin Tom, who was one year ahead of us, saw Wesley and me, arm-in-arm, coming down the hall and wanted to know if we wanted to ride over to their farm on Monday—the first day of our summer break. "Come on over, and we can ride hogs."

"Ride hogs?" I asked. That was a new one to me and to Wesley.

Tom said, "Yea, they always take off running, and some squeal like crazy. It's lots of fun and don't hurt the pig."

Wesley looked at me as though if I agreed he would too. So we both rode our bikes the three or so miles from our own farms over to Tom's on Monday morning. We got right to the hog ridin', and I must admit it was fun. These were big enough hogs to easily carry our small bodies, and they were so used to people you could walk right up to them. I don't know how often Tom rode hogs but you might have thought, as smart as hogs are, that they would have spotted trouble when they saw he was bringing two other boys with him.

Sometimes we could only go one at a time and sometimes we could get three lined up close enough we could take off like we were racing.

When that would happen Tom would yell out, "And they're off!"

He was also right that the hogs needed no prompting to take off. They would barrel-ass across the barn, I guess hoping the speed would have us sliding off their back—which it usually did. Every once in a while one would squeal the whole way. If you've never heard a pig squeal up close, you can't quite imagine the frequencies and decibels involved.

I had never seen Wesley quite as loose and happy as he was that day. We had such a hoot riding hogs, I suggested they come over to our farm sometime, and both said they would. As it turned out, "sometime" was just after we'd finished baling straw.

As before when we were all assembled, we wasted no time getting to it. I'd told Mom and Dad they were coming over on Tuesday, but I didn't disclose the actual agenda. I wasn't trying to hide anything. It just didn't occur to me it would matter one way or the other. Mom made cinnamon rolls for us so the only thing that delayed our hog riding was each having a couple of her rolls in the kitchen before heading out to the barn.

Our hog rides that day were short-lived. Dad was out working on the combine when he heard the first hog squeal. He wouldn't have had a second thought about it as it doesn't take much to get a hog to squeal, even when boys aren't trying to ride 'em. When the squealing started to persist more than he thought was normal, he headed to the barn so he could see what was going on. He took one look over the gate and hollered, "What the Sam Hill do you think you boys are doing?"

Tom said, "Riding hogs!"

I thought it best not to say anything. Wesley certainly wasn't going to say anything. You could see him quickly withdrawing as was his nature at the slightest chastisement.

50

Dad said, "If I could get one of those hogs to ride your back I would, and you could see if it's any fun then! You might hurt them hogs. I don't want anymore hog riding out of you boys. Am I understood?"

Then I knew it was my turn to respond, "Yes, Dad."

He went back to working on the combine, and we moved our adventures into the straw mow. We decided we'd build a "fort" and a long tunnel to get into it. Ultimately this would require flashlights, so I went to the shop and grabbed one for each of us. Then we got some boards from the wood pile and took those up into the mow. We started taking bales out of the middle of the stack so we had a hole about five feet deep. Then Wesley and I laid the boards across the top, spaced out just enough to hold more bales so we could put one layer deep as the roof of the fort. While we did this, Tom started opening up the tunnel we would use which just required moving the top layer of bales to create a tunnel one bale wide, and covering it back up by laying the bales crosswise across the top. When we had our roof on, we helped him finish the tunnel which went all the way across the mow.

We were about to find out if any of us were claustrophobic. Since we didn't know what that was at that point, it probably helped our psyche to just turn on the flash light and start off through the tunnel. We were pleased with our achievement and mostly sat there just admiring it. We would go back and forth through the tunnel for the fun of it and even carried a couple of our cats back in there with us. They didn't seem to mind us carrying them in through the tunnel but once back there, they didn't seem nearly as impressed with the fort as we were. Together they took off back through the tunnel to freedom as we would do as well soon enough. With our barn adventures complete, we hit the bikes and went peddling up and down the road before Tom and Wesley peddled their way home. Though we didn't think anything of it, Wesley never invited us to his farm that summer—or any other. That July day on the Kibler farm was the end of the three of us having any adventures together.

Wesley and I mostly parted company as pals when the consolidation came—as their farm was north of the dividing line and ours south. All it takes is a line on the map to divide people. I still saw him some because we continued to have our township's 4-H club, and we were both in 4-H through our senior year. He would always take a lamb to the fair and, like all the other Shudels and Kiblers, I always took a steer.

He was the one and only boy I came near to being intimate with in any way until Miles. Once on a 4-H camping trip, the two of us were sleeping in a pup tent. It was pretty hot so neither of us were in our sleeping bags; we both had them unzipped, and we just laid on top of them. Dad and we boys never had pajamas. We slept in our briefs in the summer and long-johns in the winter. That night both Wesley and I slipped off our jeans and t-shirts and went to bed in our underwear. I could never sleep on my back or my stomach and have always spent the night rolling from one side to the other.

Sometime in the middle of the night, when I was lying with my back towards him, I awoke to his body up against mine. At first I figured he'd just rolled over in his sleep, and I laid still for a minute to see if he would roll back over. I began to sense he was awake. I could feel the flesh of his chest against my back, his crotch on my backside and his legs bent into my legs. We were spooning. I lay there hoping he didn't realize I was awake. Then I realized he was sobbing ever so softly trying mightily to be unheard. I didn't even know what I was feeling sorry for at that moment, but I felt enormous pity for him all of a sudden. I didn't know whether to roll over and hug him or just leave him as he was. I had no instinct to be cruel to him. In fact my instinct, if I could have trusted it, was to take my right arm, find his and pull it into my chest. Our bodies are drawn to this pleasure of flesh against flesh, and I knew my body was experiencing a pleasure it never had before. A few minutes later, he rolled back over, and we never spoke of it.

That is one of the biggest regrets of my life. Maybe my still body was comfort enough for what he needed at that moment. Maybe he knew I was awake and was glad I let him be. Maybe he wanted some affection I never offered. Maybe I didn't have to even move—just let him know I was awake and talk to him as gently as I could. Maybe he would have opened up about the abuse he knew at home. I've wondered over the years if that was the one and only chance I had to be for him what he needed in that moment, and I failed him. I would never know.

After 4-H, I would never see him again or have any contact with him. As far as I know he never married. I did learn the rest of their family story when one of Graber girls went to his dad's funeral.

Like us, they were Mennonite. They went to a different church in the county where most of their relatives went. So far as I know, we were in no way related even distantly. The Grabers, on Marie's side, were some shirttail relation which is why they went to the funeral.

The funeral started as any would, but as soon as the minister finished his remarks about the grief of the family and the merits of the father as a good Christian man, Wesley got up from the front pew where he was seated and went straight to the pulpit. This was not part of the order of service. For a moment his eyes just scanned back and forth across the large families of aunts and uncles seated in the first few rows.

Then he started in. "I can't stand here and pretend this man was the saint you all want to convince yourselves he was." Moving his index finger back and forth across those rows of aunts and uncles he said, "Every single one of you knew that man was an alcoholic and a mean drunk. Every single one of you knew the cruelty he inflicted on his wife and his children. Every scar I have on my body came from that man. Every inappropriate touch to my sisters' bodies came from that man. Every slap our mother endured came from that man. Every one of you *knew* it, and not a single one of you ever did a *damn* thing to stop it."

He had brought the darkness of that home into the light whether they liked it or not. At that point, his mother and sisters walked up to him on the platform, passing the casket of that abusive man, and they hugged each other and wept mightily together until finally his mother turned to those assembled and said, "Please leave now."

Only the minister and the two men from the funeral home stayed behind—both standing outside the church. His mother went to talk with them and told the minister nothing else was required of him. She told the two men from the funeral home, "Take him and put him in the ground. And no, we will not be ordering a headstone. He can lie in an unmarked grave. Wesley finally had the courage for us all to tell the truth about this man."

And as our Graber friend and neighbor recounted, "That day, and that bold facing of the truth, marked the beginning of their healing."

Chapter Fourteen

As I reflect on the bully and Wesley, there is no telling what other hidden stories were buried in our childhood school days. Mostly, it all seemed like it operated on a scale from benign to joyous. We knew all the teachers and their families and they knew all of us. Our class size was usually only twenty to near thirty.

Even for the seventh- and eighth-graders, we didn't have any real competitive sports. Our gym was also the cafeteria. We might play kickball or basketball when the tables were folded up. We played softball or touch football at recess. The rest of the time was spent on swings, see-saws, monkey bars and hopscotch when we weren't off on some imaginary game of our own making. In music class we square danced to music on a record player—yes, dancing Mennonites. When I told Mom about it, she wanted to know how I liked it. I said the girl I danced with had sweaty hands. She just laughed.

Because of the township school, my cousins were mostly just more kids at the school. The only difference were the times we'd get together as the whole family, going to church together and helping on each other's farms.

All that changed when I was in sixth grade. "Progress" mandated by the State Board of Education suggested the bigger the school the better the education. After all, what could a little township school offer its students other than an egalitarian and imaginative education? The Amish would maintain their own schools. The Mennonites were always integrated into the community including the public schools. So when someone looked at a map of the township, they drew an arbitrary line that sent everyone north of the line to one school and everyone south to another. True, we were going to end up in one of those high schools anyway, but we gave up a lot in the process. Now rather than classes, we were in "sections" with teachers we didn't know, who could not connect much beyond a few families with any familiarity. The less-gifted students no longer had their friendship support system and only fell further behind. Friendships migrated into cliques—and neighbors and cousins landed into grade-specific clusters with little interaction anymore.

I'm not trying to sell these as terrible schools. Sure, they afforded opportunities for band, choir, sports and foreign language classes our township school didn't offer. But I do know that talking with those old alum of the township school decades later, we all felt a sense of loss—and not gain—in our new experience in the larger schools. It's no wonder huge public schools are rife with problems. I suppose it's a lost cause to hope schools would ever return to a small-school model—though there are some in France and Switzerland doing it. I will always think my education would have only been richer had our township school gone the other way and included high school. The building is long gone. Now it's just another cornfield.

It will always be a mystery to me how a mostly Mennonite community could have a high school whose mascots were called the "Blue Devils." It must have been because of those Lutherans or Catholics or Methodists who had churches in town. There was only one Mennonite church actually within the "city" limits—and just barely so on the east edge of town. All the others were like Hope Mennonite—country churches, as was the one Church of the Brethren where Rose attended.

If I fell more towards the benign end of the scale at the township school—never being a great lover of school—I definitely moved to the negative quadrant when I got to the "new and improved" school that consolidation had deemed a must. It was especially bad those first couple years. I absolutely dreaded getting up and going to school. I wasn't alone. There was one boy from the township school who lived back down a long lane, and when the school bus stopped, some days he just wouldn't get on with his brothers and sisters. I didn't think that was going to go over at all in the Kibler household and never tried it—tempted though I was. Really, I'm not sure why I hated it to the degree I did. All my cousins, other Hope Mennonite kids and half my township friends were on the south side of the dividing line, so I knew loads of people at school. I wasn't unpopular or bullied. I must have been outgoing enough because my seventh-grade teacher asked one day if I thought I was the ambassador of goodwill. She did not mean that as a compliment but rather as a chastisement of my talking in class over paying attention to her. The only good graces I had with her were helping with anything technical. She liked to show films, which were on reels in those days, and she couldn't load the film projector to save her life. She always had me set up anything A/V-related for her. It's probably the only thing that kept me on the lower side of a "B" average in her class instead of the lower "C" I might well have deserved.

My disdain for school did not follow the bell curve we studied in math class. While at the township school the graph would have registered near zero on the "x" axis from one year to the next, the first year with the "Blue Devils" it shot up like the Spanish Flu infection—and other than a slight variance at different times over the years, it remained flat at that elevated level never coming back down anywhere near zero. All I can really attribute this to were these—liking outdoors more than in, small groups of people over large, a general dislike of conformity, and learning proclivities not accommodated by textbook instruction (not understood by me until much later in life).

I hadn't really noticed in the township school whether I had any talent or not. I just never thought about it. Our music teacher did have me sing the second verse of *Away in a Manger* at the school Christmas program. As a class we sat on the floor, legs folded up, as the class sang the first verse—and then the little boy soprano stood and sang.

The cattle are lowing, the poor baby wakes,
But little Lord Jesus, no crying he makes.
I love thee, Lord Jesus! look down from the sky,
And stay by my cradle till morning is nigh.

Then I sat back down with my classmates as we finished the third verse. I never knew why she picked me. I was the only soloist that evening.

At the Blue Devils' school I would join the choir and small ensembles and sing in the chorus for musicals, but I never liked singing solos. I would solo a lot more than I ever wanted to thanks to the guilt piled on by my Grandma Shudel and Mom and Dad. Oddly, the only solo I ever remember not being a nervous wreck when I sang it was that second verse in the second grade. Maybe it was the comfort of the township school, lost when I joined the Blue Devils.

The solo singing I did do earned me a taste of bullying—mild though it was. A couple boys started calling me a sissy and making effeminate gestures with their hands in a limp wrist from their outstretched arms as I'd walk by. The apparent cause of this was the voice lessons I was taking once a week—that again were Mom and Dad's idea, not mine! Maybe these two boys had some premonition of my sexuality I had not yet awakened to—though I doubt it. They were like some of the Catholic boys who would attach that label to all us Mennonite boys.

If there is an upside to being gay and Mennonite, I would have to say it is having to deal with early on with being different and getting nasty comments about being a CO. This was my first taste of bullying and it happened soon after I arrived at the Blue Devils' school. I had little Catholic boys, younger than me, calling me a CO like it was the nastiest thing imaginable even before I knew what a CO was. We didn't use the term in any public way at Hope Mennonite.

Truthfully, by the time I was growing up in the Mennonite Church we were becoming pretty watered-down Mennonites. The strict prohibitions to instruments in church were beginning to fall away. Some congregations (at least with Mennonite in the name) allowed their members to serve in the military. They all appeared to be "all in" on adapting new technologies for farming and factories. They voted. A few flags began appearing in front of their homes—not a common thing, but not without examples in our county.

So, while at the township school we all seemed to fit and fit in, at the Blue Devils' school, I was now labeled both sissy and CO. Such fun!

Chapter Fifteen

One day I came home from school after junior high wrestling practice and couldn't find Spicer anywhere. Mom informed me, "Wayne found her dead out on the barn floor." When I went out to the barn to see her, she wasn't there. I looked all over. It wasn't like her to go in the barn anyway but I'd guessed, like old dogs do, she knew it was her time and went off to die. I found Wayne in the farrowing house and asked where Spicer was. I couldn't believe what I heard next.

"I took her out in the field with me and dropped her off the back of the tractor to plow her under." He said this as though this was the only thing to be done.

I just couldn't believe it, and I must confess when he came back home in that box from that stupid war, I thought to myself, "Maybe we should take you out and plow you under." I might just as well be honest about it in the telling. I'm not sure I ever really grieved Wayne's death. He was to me little more than just an older, ornery brother for whom I'm hard-pressed to think of one kind thing he ever did. Perhaps such an ungenerous notion is just my own blindness towards him.

A schoolmate offered me one of their pups—another small mixed breed of what I was never sure. I named him Dibs and was disappointed when Mom announced she didn't want another house dog—which Spicer had been. I set out to build him a well-insulated dog house with a carpeted flap for a door. He seemed to like being outside okay, and I would bring him in the house for short periods from time to time but never overnight. Even though he wasn't a house dog, when I loaded up the car for college, poor Dibs wanted to get in the car with me. He'd never ridden in a car since the day I brought him home. It surprised Mom and Dad as well as me.

Mom said, "He seems to think he should be going to college with you."

I guess he should have—though dorms rules being what they are, that was not a possibility. After I left, he took to chasing cars when they'd pass on the road. After a couple years of that, he got hit one day and was hurt pretty badly. Dad took him into the basement of the house and tried to nurse him back to health, but he only lived into the next day. Dad gave this second dog a proper Christian burial in the backyard. No burial by plow this time around.

Chapter Sixteen

Once in high school, somehow the choir director persuaded me to sing the *National Anthem* at the opening of a home basketball game. He was rather egalitarian in this regard—picking a different student for every game. I dreaded it but did it. I probably should have thought to ask, "Are you sure sissies are approved to sing it?"

I didn't tell Mom or Dad I had been asked to do it. They didn't know until they heard it on the radio, as the game was broadcast on the local FM station.

The announcer came on. "Please stand for the *National Anthem* sung by senior August Kibler."

I thought not telling them was a pretty good trick on my part. It never occurred to me they would even have the game on!

For some reason they didn't agree—my dad saying as soon as I came through the door later that night, "Didn't you think we'd want to be there to hear you?"

And me responding, "Couldn't imagine why you would wanna be."

It was the first time he referred to me as an "independent little shit," but it wouldn't be the last.

I think I pulled it out of the fire a bit with my final comeback to our exchange when I said, "Probably am, but you did raise your children to be independent." What he might not have liked in the context of that comment he had to accept as simple fact.

I also hated every sport I ever tried. Well, that's not quite accurate. I liked wrestling, but I didn't like most of my fellow wrestlers who were of the school's rough and tumble and had a habit of trying to outdo each other's manhood by eating raw eggs—which was supposed to prove something. Still gags me to think of it! Maybe it pumped up their testosterone—they had plenty of that or pretended they did at any rate. And I hated meets and tournaments with fans screaming in the bleachers. In those cases, I always knew I was going to lose before I ever went out onto the mat. The only hope I had at such events was coming against some boy who hated it as much as me and would be weaker than me from growing up in town instead of on a farm.

It was certainly true that any lack of strength was not the problem. I was strong as an ox and always had enough meat on my bones to lift about anything. Had I taken them on, those Catholic town boys and the two boys who called me a sissy would have been flattened in an instant. My older and bigger brother never wrestled, and I could pin him in about two minutes no matter how many times he tried to take me on. I lacked some support structure I apparently had an inherent need for, but perhaps more than that it was the idea of competition—there must be a winner and there must be a loser. That just never sat right with me. As bad as it was with my wrestling, it was as bad or worse the one time I tried football. I just hoped I would get to ride the bench with some of the in-town, weaker kids who were on the team. Cursed be those coaches who thought every kid had to play every game! Oh, I know that's supposed to be a good thing—didn't seem like it at the time.

Maybe if we'd had soccer back in those days. There's a sport where missing a goal is more the norm than making one; you don't have to wear a helmet or padded uniform while you bash your body to concussion levels; soccer uniforms look a whole lot more comfortable in public than those wrestling uniforms; and all those boys get to jump up into each other's arms with every little success. That last one especially always looked pretty good to me!

The most fun I had in high school was when the musical would roll around every year—so long as I didn't have any onstage role. Mostly, I loved the behind-the-scenes work—and my junior and senior years I was basically the foreman for any and all set work. My Kibler-Shudel construction skills were both needed and wildly appreciated by the choir director who also directed the musical. My senior year he appointed me as a student director, and that was the first foretaste I had that perhaps I could be a music teacher or choral director. In fact, I enjoyed it so much, and it influenced me so heavily, I couldn't quite ever think about any other occupation I would be good at. I might have considered construction were it not for everyone thinking anyone with average-to-better grades had to go to college—a problem that persists or has gotten worse since my day. Only later would I learn about the strong connection the Swiss still have to mentorships and apprenticeships. Those were nowhere in sight at the Blue Devils' school—at least not that I could see.

Dating was not really a thing for me in high school. I had my little, mixed clique of guy friends and girl friends but there were no romantic notions passing among the bunch of us. During one of the musicals I came close to having a girlfriend, but she proved too "hot to trot" for me. She loved French kissing and somehow I slithered away soon enough from that brief encounter. The only other time I tried to date was when I asked a girl in our class to go to the junior prom. She quite literally laughed out loud and turned me down. She shook her head and said, "No," and walked away.

I don't know what was funny about it. I remember standing in the hall of the school feeling pretty foolish. I had figured that unless she already had a date, she would go. She was a very attractive girl and was someone I'd known long enough that I certainly didn't deserve that reaction. My high school annual can confirm, I was pretty good looking amongst my Blue Devils classmates. I was even more surprised by who she did go to the prom with. I took one look and thought to myself, "Okay." Not who I would have picked for me or her, but there's no accounting for taste.

Maybe it was God doing the laughing and she just happened to be there for the voice box needed. (I hadn't yet clued in on how good God's sense of humor was.) It certainly did make me wonder for the first time if those boys calling me a sissy was the general consensus of my schoolmates. It also marked the end of my dating adventures. I'd stick to group activities from then on until Miles and I met those years later. I suppose this was a classic form of denial of one's sexuality at that point, but that was not something I was ready to give any consideration to anytime soon.

Chapter Seventeen

I wasn't persuaded that farming was the life for me. The livelihood of the small, family farmer was being choked year-to-year by inflation, high interest rates, bad weather and the roller coaster markets. So early on, I learned that farming wasn't for the faint of heart. Also, I seemed to have a knack for getting a tractor stuck or some shear pin breaking off whatever I was operating. I even literally was driving our 4020 John Deere tractor when the entire assembly carrying the front wheels fell off when I went over a furrow in the field near the barn. They flung around and went crashing into the radiator with the front of the tractor sinking into the dirt. Was this a sign from God I shouldn't be a farmer? God seemed to be already saying—don't date yet!

About the same time the wheels fell off the tractor, I was going through the only real anger phase I had in my life. I'm not exactly sure what brought it on, but I know what aggravated it too many times.

Conrad Graber had long farrowed his own hogs. He had a few square pens filled with straw where he would move the individual sow when it was time to birth. He kept the sows a long time. They were huge. I liked to watch him slop the sows which was just a mixture of their corn meal and water—probably some supplements; I don't recall.

Dad's approach was much higher-tech. When the farrowing house first was going up, I was so impressed. It had ventilation for summer and heated floors for winter. While we'd be freezing in the old farm house, the hogs had seventy-degree, comfort-controlled, heated flooring. When finished, even though it only held twelve sows, I realized just how industrial it really was. The stanchion the sow was put into was not much wider than she and long enough to allow her shit to fall behind her. The pen overall had low, solid, galvanized panels that formed an area on each side of the stanchion for the newborn pigs. The concept was if the sow could only get up and down while she was in there then she'd be less likely to lie down on one of her piglets—though this still happened on occasion as there's only so much delicacy a 200-plus pound sow can muster trying to lie back down. (Dad always sold ours off before they got as big as Conrad's as the "experts" said such old sows were past their "full productive use.")

I couldn't recall Conrad's pens smelling any different than the rest of the barn. This "industrial farrowing house" had a whole new smell all its own. My Mom and I were of one mind on this—it was disgusting! It was so strong the minute you walked in, even if you turned right around you stunk to high heaven. I've never smelled anything like it before or since. With the ventilation I couldn't quite understand why it stayed so consistently strong, but it did regardless of the season of year.

With three groups of sows, it was rarely empty. One group moved out as another group moved in. I had the delightful chore of going in every afternoon—seven days a week—to clean out each of the twelve pens. There was no straw ever used in these pens, so everyday you had to hoe out all the manure from anywhere in the pen, pull it into the aisle and then push the accumulating piles to one end where an auger carried it outside. I never did this chore with any love for it or its occupants. I detested it!

One afternoon, for whatever had come before it to anger me already—probably either something one of my sisters or brother had done or maybe something at the Blue Devils—I entered the farrowing house madder than a hornet. I started my pen cleaning cursing the place as I went. In one pen a piglet no bigger than a half-grown rabbit got straddled over the top of my hoe, and I gave him a good fling up to the front of the stall. I carried on with my rage-full cleaning until I was finally glad to be out of that stinking place.

The next night I was back to more of my normal disdain, with the outrage having mercifully subsided. When I got to the pen where I'd given the piglet a good piece of my mind, there was a small dead pig. I was instantly flooded with shame!

Losing newborn pigs in their first days isn't unusual. In fact, another of my chores was burying, or cremating in winter when the ground was too frozen, any pigs who had died. I was certainly used to dealing with dead pigs. But by all that is right in this world, something told me I had killed that pig with my rage. Whether I really did or not, I could never know, but it changed me forever. The remorse I felt over the death of such a helpless creature made me vow then that I would never let my anger strike out at another living creature. That pig would not die in vain. I learned patience in an instant that would travel with me throughout my life—though many would try my patience. And I would never strike anyone or anything for any reason—a vow I've kept to the present. When Miles asked me about how I stay so calm, I figured he deserved the whole story. I ended the telling of it with this.

"The story is told of a man who had great patience. Someone asked him one day at work, 'How do you stay so calm.'

"He answered, 'Because I like dogs.'

"'Pardon?' She asked.'

"He explained, 'I used to take my frustration home and snap at my wife. She then would snap at the children, and one day I saw our youngest boy go into the backyard and kick the dog. I decided then I had to find a better way.'"

Then I said, "When someone asks me how is it that I am so patient, I just smile at them; but inside I hear the answer loud and clear—because of one dead pig."

Chapter Eighteen

The best advice my dad ever gave me—and no, I didn't take it—was, "You should go to college to study landscape engineering and design."

Perhaps if the art teacher at the Blue Devils school hadn't given me a "C-" in the class when my friends all got an "A," I might have thought I had some gift of creativity. I did not. In my day, there was no computer-aided design software—so any interest I might have had in design or architecture was quickly dismissed, as my "C-" in art class only validated a lack of creative talent.

At the time of Dad's suggestion I thought, "How would I ever make a living doing that?" I did like plants and my hands in the dirt. I would go back to the woods and dig up seedlings of trees and replant them in our yard. I even would go to the Grabers with a tree or two. If they didn't want them, they were kind enough to pretend they did as I proceeded to dig a hole where they instructed me to put the latest transplant.

One Sunday when I was still pretty young, I was out digging up the iris bed which went around our house. I wanted to thin them out, replanting all of them to have more irises the next season. I'd never seen Mom, Dad or my siblings take on this task. It just looked to me like it needed doing, and I did it. Grandma Shudel came over that afternoon in the middle of my good work. I said, "Hi, Grandma," and went right on working.

She didn't box my ears, but she did say to Mom, "Why is that boy working on that on a Sunday?"

Mom answered, "As much as he enjoys it, it isn't work to him."

I thought that was pretty wise of her to recognize the joy I had with such things in nature. This was to become a lifelong passion if not a vocation. I never did get any income as a landscaper, but once Miles and I had the duplex, I resumed my passion. I never hired or intend to hire anyone, so long as the old body can go on, to "maintain" all the flower beds, rose garden and manicured lawn. I'd go one step further than Aunt Ilah and get a motorized lawn mower, though never a riding one—and I would cut it as often as we had to cut hers to keep it at a length we could push that reel mower through. Now with the Jemison boys next door, I get plenty of volunteer help these days anyway. I've never offered them any money for their help. We keep such help as we keep the books on the rest of our lives together—returning gratitude for gratitude.

Dad either had some prophetic notion of the landscape industry, or I was just blind to the possibilities. Everyone we knew growing up did all their own "landscaping." There wasn't even a single mowing service that I was ever aware of at the time. That's what sons and nephews were for. By the time I graduated from Anderson, there were plenty of start-up businesses providing lawn and landscaping services, and most were making a better living than most farmers.

I suppose since he and Mom had both forced me into all that solo singing over the years, he felt my decision to go to college to study music was a fruit of their labor that they should accept as the logical progression. Though it must be said, with the emphasis on solo recitals, it took me no time changing my music major to business.

My second bout as an "independent little shit" came when I announced that I wanted to go to college at Anderson. None of us had ever heard of it, and it was not a Mennonite college. It was Church of God—also of which we'd never heard. And while Anderson was in Indiana, it was not in a town any of us had ever been to. I-69 runs around it and not through it, and so one never even sees the town as one drives along the interstate. Plenty of my schoolmates went off to good Mennonite colleges like Goshen and Bluffton. The smarter ones who couldn't afford a private school went to local state universities. That's what I should have done given I couldn't afford a private liberal arts college either, but their size intimidated me. I'm not sure my brain was processing on all cylinders when it came to making either career or college decisions.

Anderson had come to a college day that the local counties had sponsored for high school seniors. They were there with a large, color-photo booth display. One of the pictures was of the Park Place church steeple that lined up so perfectly at the end of one of the streets on campus; and one was of the new Decker Hall with its impressive cantilever design. I persuaded a couple of classmates to join me for a visit to the campus. I loved the campus and the church. To my surprise my application was accepted and so, asserting my latest act of independence, I set off on my new adventure.

One of my companions on the visit went there as well. As she would point out years later, "You are the only person in the world I went to school with for 16 years." You see, she too was from the old township school, and their farm was south of the dividing line just like ours.

I was never sure how the Kibler homestead was going to stay in the family. Family farms were dying faster than their inhabitants. I rather hoped one of us could keep it plugging along. And I rather hoped it wasn't my younger sister, Kathy.

I was always of the opinion that one or both of my sisters were the primary contributors to our sometimes unruly house. My older sister Deb blamed the younger sister. This was, in fact, confirmed when the higgledy-piggledy Kathy married. When we would visit her home, it looked like a tornado had just gone through. Somehow my brother, Wayne, Deb and I all grew up knowing how to cook, and do laundry and basic "maintenance" that life on the farm requires. Kathy somehow escaped domestic duties in her childhood more than the rest of us, and it caught up with her when she began her own family. Perhaps out of weariness of hearing the Kiblers fuss about her domestic shortcomings, she eventually improved, becoming a little better housekeeper and a good baker—though whenever she was in the kitchen, it always appeared as though five people were in there at once leaving a mess for someone else to clean up. She certainly didn't adopt my practice of washing and tidying as you go.

When Mom and Dad first talked about giving up farming, Miles and I entertained the notion of leaving Boone to buy the farm and take it over. Miles would have to get a job in town to give us something to live off of and pay the note on the property, and I would be the "chief operating officer" of the farm, which meant doing everything there was to do in the barns and in the fields. I was sure I would also have to draw on my carpenter skills to earn a little on the side. Dad was most discouraging of such a plan. By then, he'd become convinced operating an 80-acre farm was an exercise in futility. Specialty organic farms would try and in some cases appear to make it, but they were not commonplace, and he questioned whether they could really make it financially over the long haul.

Miles and I finally decided this was more of a romantic notion than a viable way forward, and we were better off staying in Boone, with its cooler summers, and sticking to the much less volatile livelihoods we both were lucky to have. To start farming at this point would be a precarious venture towards a hope for an agrarian livelihood —so this one time in my life, I *would* take Dad's advice.

I said to Miles, "I can see us sinking blood, sweat and tears into this—the same place where I could get any implement stuck, sheer off every pin and fling the front wheels of the tractor into the radiator—and then wonder what went wrong."

Miles said, "You'll want me working two jobs to keep it all afloat."

To which I said, "Well, I might finally go to the doctor. He'll ask, 'What can I do for you?' And I'll say, 'I'm here for euthanasia.'"

Miles responded, "Boone soundin' better all the time."

With Wayne gone and our own farming notions dismissed once and for all, when Mom and Dad were ready to give it up, my oldest sister, Deb, along with her husband, Bob, moved onto the old home place. I'm not sure I can call it the family farm anymore. They now rent the land out, and the buildings are all empty except for a couple horses they keep.

Dad loved draft horses back in the day and liked harness racing too, but he wasn't impressed with their horses. "What are you going to do with them. They'll eat and drink and shit and not do any work to make it all even out. I don't see you even ridin' 'em much."

Bob responded, "They are your daughter's very expensive lawn ornaments. She just likes to look at them out on the grass the few weeks it's bright green."

This prompted Dad to look at his daughter, as up to that point he'd assumed this folly was Bob's doing. He said to her, "I thought I raised you with more sense than that," adding his two cents to all such notions: "A fool and his money."

Dad's childhood with Grandpa Kibler was indeed a time of farming by draft horse. None of my family roots would resist the adaptation of electricity or technology as the hard-core Amish would. Still, they farmed by draft horse since few if any farmers had tractors yet.

For as long as I can remember, Dad farmed both the homeplace and the farm that had belonged to Uncle Christian and Aunt Ilah, whose owner lived in the house and rented out the land.

Dad always said, "The farmer started losing money when he had to borrow for equipment instead of just stock, and because of lights on tractors."

I asked what lights on tractors had to do with it.

He responded, "Because then the farmer didn't need to quit before sundown to get the horses put up and fed. He could work into the night and glutted the market with all his 'increased productivity.'"

That led me to ask, "Then why did you buy tractors? The Amish up the road never did."

He said, "I could say it's as simple as they have at least half-a-dozen boys to help work the farm and don't need all that horsepower by fire like I do, or I could say it's because they were always more for standing still while we were more for moving forward. I will say, once you've gone down the road of modernizing the farm, it doesn't look like there's a path going back —it's been plowed under and 'progress' planted on top of it. Unfortunately more and more, it's the government and the corporations that tell you what progress is and how you supposedly can't afford not to buy it. 'Get big or get out,' as they put it. I'm finally old enough to take the latter half of their directive and get out."

Mom might have been content to move into town, but Dad wasn't ready to do that, although staying put, he thought, was more than they needed to deal with at their age. They found a place closer to town where the buildings were being sold off, which consisted of a small house and one small barn. That suited him for keeping a couple hogs all the time and Mom keeping a few chickens. No equine lawn ornaments in sight. The only implement

Dad took from the old homeplace was his John Deere riding mower.

I said to Miles, "If Mom listens to him while he's out there mowing, she'll probably hear him singing his favorite song, *Home on the Range.* I've thought for a long time maybe he was supposed to be a rancher instead of a farmer—but then he never was one to spend time worrying about what might have been. I guess singing about the open range is enough for him."

To be fair to Bob and Deb, they did care for the old Kibler place. Bob is president of the largest bank in the county and inherited bank stocks from his father, who inherited plenty from his grandfather who was one of the bank's founders. Deb had a successful flower shop. They plowed money into maintaining all the buildings, and since it was technically still a family farm—even though the land was rented out—they had a Centennial medallion from the State. The only building they ever tore down was that farrowing house which had no historical context to the rest of the buildings, and I was wholly grateful to see it razed. The farm was one of those picture-perfect farmsteads that people would stop on the road to take a picture of even if it wasn't really a farm anymore—it looks like what we want farms to look like. The fine, two-story, red brick house looked like it had just been built with all the character of yesteryear. The barns with their handsome stone foundations and red siding with white trim always looked like the painter had just finished. Yes, those driving by would even stop and take pictures of those two horses out on the green pasture.

The Shudel farm, less than a half-mile down the road, didn't fare nearly as well. When Grandma Shudel died, the siblings agreed to auction off both the homestead and the eighty acres to the East. When the new owner saw land prices shooting up a few years later, he sold off the acreage to one of the large operators in the county who quickly had all the woods on both farms clear-cut and set to the plow. The owner also sold off the buildings, rather on the cheap, to get rid of them. Then he and his wife retired to Long Boat Key in Florida. The next owners didn't know how to hold a paintbrush, apparently, or patch a roof and soon everything took on a shabby feel. They pulled in a mobile home next to the old clapboard-sided house for whatever relative was staying there as well.

Deb said, "It's pretty obvious that when anything might need a new roof, they are going to let it go and just move in trailers as needed."

She was right. The last time I was in Ohio, the barn had collapsed into itself and you would need a machete to even get to it. There were half a dozen old, dead cars and trucks in the yard, several windows broken in the house as it heads towards its own eventual collapse if fire doesn't take it first, and two single-wides and one double-wide now the domiciles for its careless inhabitants —each already looking like their destiny will be like that of the house and barn, to die in place from lack of care.

Such is life in the unzoned countryside. One showplace just down the road from a trash heap—a growing disease of our time.

Chapter Nineteen

The Bonneville loaded up and with my sad farewell to Dibs, we headed to Anderson. I wouldn't have a car on campus my freshman year. When Mom and Dad first helped me carry everything into my dorm room, and I watched as their car drove away, for the first time I realized how singularly I had come to this decision to go to a school a few hours from the farm and now the "independent little shit" really was on his own.

Wayne hadn't cut it even a semester even though he went to a Mennonite college. I was determined not to repeat that. Through work study, I had a job in the school cafeteria where I was more than useful to the food service manager. He quickly saw that I knew my way around a kitchen and that I would work harder than most. I got a lot of extra hours from my allotted time for the week because I would stay on Saturday and do heavy cleaning of all the drink machines and walk-in coolers. When they needed a hand in the dishwasher room, I would jump off my duties keeping the salad bar, condiment bar and drinks bar stocked to help them with the mad rush of trays coming back on the conveyor belt towards the end of breakfast or lunch.

I also worked the worst schedule I think you could have. Monday to Saturday breakfast—which meant traipsing through the cold, snow and dark to get there by 6:15 much like my chore schedule back on the farm—and Saturday and Sunday lunch. As with all my jobs in life I was never late and always at least 10 minutes early.

It was the first job I had where I realized how invisible food service and custodial staff are on a college campus—and, we must grant, in every office building and airport. You are rarely if ever thanked or acknowledged. People seem to go out of their way to leave things as messy as possible for you to clean up behind them. If you are trying to carry something in, they make no effort at getting out of your way. Yes, this was a Christian college and yes, I recognized a level of self-absorption that was new to me.

One time, I came out of my invisible status at a busy Saturday lunch—the cafeteria full. The milk for the milk machines came in some kind of bag that holds four or five gallons and had to be lifted up into the cooler, with a little, rubber teat-like tube that hangs down the bottom and then is cut off. The weight of the handle pinches off the valve that is just a piece of metal pressing against the tube. I knew it was always a precarious endeavor lifting the bag into place.

On this particular day, this particular bag had a blowout where the tube connects to the bag just as I hoisted it into place. The gallons of milk came pouring out all over me and all over the floor. Instantly, my Christian brothers and sisters broke into applause for my mishap—some even giving me a standing ovation. Fortunately, the strong Kibler-Shudel stock allowed me to ignore them, go get a mop and bucket and another bag of milk without ever bursting into tears. If I were a little more worldly, I probably would have flipped them a middle finger. I'll admit, the thought crossed my mind—but was dismissed as I knew for sure that would have Grandma Shudel boxing my ears from her grave!

If I had a highlight academically my freshman year it had to be my Old Testament class. I'm pretty sure the near-retired professor was about the least popular on campus—at least those aligned with the school of theology—but he was number one in my book. All the students I knew thought he was too eccentric—apparently a bad thing. At any rate, I can say I'd never read the Old or New Testament the same way again.

I especially loved when he would take us out of the classroom on beautiful fall days. We would sit under a huge old sycamore overlooking the pretty valley that runs through the center of the campus, and he would read Psalms to us—not standing over us like some great sage, but sitting on the ground with us, just as I imagined Jesus did so many times as he shared the parables with his listeners.

As much as I wanted to join the Park Place choir, my Sunday morning schedule precluded me from attending at all on Sunday mornings. I would go on Sunday evenings, but there was no choir at those evening services. And although I liked working in the cafeteria (more or less), the pay for work study was not helping me much financially for all the labor going into it. So when I went home that summer after my freshman year, I saved all my wages from working on the construction crew to buy a used Torino which I took back with me to college. I went back a couple weeks before school started to look for a job off-campus. I lucked into a part-time job with a commercial contractor. Instead of wood I was mostly framing with metal studs, which do have the benefit of being light weight with no warps or twists unlike some of the lumber one gets ahold of. I could earn four times what I could make on campus.

It did force me to take Tuesday-Thursday evening classes every semester, but the contractor was kind enough to accommodate my class schedule as much as was reasonable to do—a good fortune I would have throughout the rest of my "academic life." It was also year-round work. That Freshman summer was my last summer to ever go back to Ohio for any extended period.

With this new work schedule, my sophomore year I was able to join the college choir and the Park Place choir. In those days, the music department was co-located in the church. Most of our concerts were in the sanctuary with the wonderful Casavant pipe organ. Park Place had a wonderful organist who also taught organ for the college. This was quite a shift from our four-part a cappella singing at Hope Mennonite. But I already knew I would love it.

We had a small stereo record player at home—which would draw mockery these days—and a small collection of records, mostly Christmas albums. I seemed to be the only one in the family fixated on them. I would sit in the living room with only the Christmas tree lights on and play the records over and over. A couple had pipe organ for accompaniment to the choir singing. One in particular that I remember was the Mormon Tabernacle Choir, which had a cover with the huge choir and that organ behind them. I was hooked!

A couple friends of mine were studying organ, and they practiced on the Casavant. I began to learn about how it all worked and where the blowers were and which stops made which sounds. I liked to "enhance" their practice with my own adaptation of registrations while they played. They didn't seem to mind.

Once when one of them was practicing, I turned it off and went and sat where I could see her reaction. Of course, the bellows took a while to give up their wind, and I was well away and sitting where I could see her and she could see me as it started to go weaker and flatter. She got a sudden panicked look on her face as though the organ had something seriously going awry. There was that mischievous self—having its fun. It worked so well on her, I had to try it on my other organ student friend—with the same enjoyable result.

We had chapel every Tuesday and Thursday morning. No classes ever interfered with that nor did my freshman work schedule. Chapel always included some singing, so my freshman year I was in Park Place every Tuesday and Thursday singing many altogether new hymns from the Church of God hymnal. I loved them! Very upbeat and fun to sing. By my sophomore year, my work schedule would interfere with chapel more than not, and I had to get an excuse from the administration to skip it. I missed it, but had little choice and made up for it by finally being able to attend on Sundays.

Both in the college choir and Park Place choir there was a young man I'd seen my freshman year but never talked to. I knew his name and that was about it. I couldn't help being interested for reasons I couldn't or wouldn't articulate at the time. Now, this young man was sitting across in the tenor section with me in the bass/baritone ranks. Really our ranges were pretty much the same. Either of us had enough range to move to the other section if needed—which it didn't seem to be. Thus it was, the tenor I would soon meet officially, Miles Bergeron, and I first became acquainted. It would only be an honest telling if I didn't state that from the start, when the baritones weren't singing and not having to keep an eye on either of the directors of these two choirs, my eyes were on others in the choir—and no one more so than on Miles. I didn't see him paying me much attention and had already classified him as super popular and not someone who would befriend me. He was always starring in some drama or musical production on campus and, unlike me, loved singing solos. Neither of us ever even spoke to each other that fall term. After all, I was just "envious" of him, and he had all the friends he wanted as best I could tell.

When the spring semester started we had our first class together, and I suppose as much out of our commonality in the choirs as anything, he sat down beside me in class and continued to do so every class day after that. He was getting friendlier and friendlier, and I was getting more and more confused by my feelings. By the time the famous choir tour came around and we went to that black church in Macon, my mind finally opened to what my heart already knew—and had known for some time. I was in love, and to my good fortune—unlike the last time I tried to have a date and got laughed off—so was the man looking back at me.

Most people see what they want to see and don't see what they don't want to see. That can be an advantage and a disadvantage. The advantage is—one can mostly just go on without anyone suspecting anything but two young men as friends. It seemed like the only one who really figured out we were more than friends was that professor of our common class. He would soon leave the college because of his own sexuality, but until then he would always give us a big grin when we came into class together—especially if we happened to be a couple minutes late as his was in the first class hour of the day.

We have dealt with the disadvantages in many ways over many years. There are always the judgmental who, it appears to me, can only construct in their narrow mind—on the most perverse level—what two men spending their time together (when sports is not involved) are up to. And of course there are the chapter-and-verse Christians who, on hearing the slightest rumor, are bound to announce to their world their concern for our souls. Mind you, they don't necessarily talk to us about our souls—just to those endangering their own by their mere association with such abominable creatures. The only difference between these two judgmental groups is that the violence of their tongues is more likely to progress to beatings and killings in the former crowd.

I never have understood the chapter-and-verse cherry-picking that goes on in Christianity. Give me a dogma you want to defend —I don't care how crazy—and I can find you chapter and verse to back it up. And in their quest for their "literal reading" of their "inerrant scriptures" they ignore, wholesale, most everything the prophets ever decried and the Sermon on the Mount postulated. If Grandpa Shudel thought the only creed needed for Hope Mennonite was—Loving God, Loving Ourselves, Loving Others, then the inerrantists' must be something along the line—worship the Bible and pray to the Mighty-Smiter to smite everyone not like us.

Or as Miles would put it, "They are dying to get to heaven just to prove they're right."

We Mennonites call that pride.

Chapter Twenty

I carried over my preference for behind-the-scenes work at Anderson as I had at the Blue Devils school. My freshman year I volunteered to help, as my schedule allowed, with any set building the drama department needed for their productions. They were thrilled to have me. One of the early projects was a set of stairs. The director wanted about a six-foot-high staircase for the set so it had to be safe and substantial. The student director, a senior, who was in charge backstage wasn't sure how to go about it and asked me for help. I gave him a bill of materials for what we'd need which he rounded up, and then I showed him how to calculate each rise and how to lay it all out with a framing square. Given its weight and proportions, it had to be made easily moveable so we included heavy-duty casters underneath, leaving the set of stairs just about half an inch off the floor—just enough to move but not enough to make the casters obvious.

While the rest of the sets were always "struck" following a production, the stairs endured as long as I was in Anderson. Every once in a while they would be rolled out for another production. I'm sure they are long gone by now, but I do wonder sometimes if by chance someone took enough care to see to them. I told Miles, perhaps if we are ever back on campus we should stop in and see.

I said, "If they are still there, we could suggest they get a small brass plaque and inscribe on it 'August Kibler Memorial Stairs.'"

He said, "I think you're supposed to be dead to be memorialized."

And I said back to him, "You know I might well be as far as their records show."

He knew what I meant by this. Years after we'd left Anderson and the Church of God over our concerns for where things were tending, some alumni publication had some article that got me all wound up. Mercifully, as is often the case, the details have left my consciousness. What it triggered from me at the time was a brief, but forthright, letter to the university telling them that I wanted to be removed from any and all correspondence. If that meant marking me as deceased in their database so as not to stumble accidentally into reactivating my record, then they should do so.

All I know is I've never heard from them again and may well "be dead to them."

While I was backstage, Miles was onstage. I'm not sure he's ever driven ten nails in his whole life. I know he couldn't cut out a set of stairs. He, of course, liked solo singing and, equally, acting, so over the years he was Jesus in *Godspell*, Tevye in *Fiddler on the Roof*, Tom Wingfield in *The Glass Menagerie*, Sky Masterson in *Guys and Dolls* and many more leading roles. As with all "stars" he had his fan club as well—mostly girls who would follow him about.

His gift as a listener along with an inherent heart of sympathy made many of the girls confide in him with all manner of things. Some he would immediately tell me about but, just as often, if it was something told in confidence, he respected their privacy absolutely. All too often those ended with the girls "falling in love" with him even though they knew such depth of intimacy was not being returned. He was as kind as anyone could be in those situations. Except for one, they always seemed to remain cordial after their confiding how they felt. When he'd tell me the latest account, I'd just shake my head and say, "Heart-breaker Bergeron."

Among his fans was one he and I would call "the stalker." This was a guy in our same class who clearly had a huge crush on Miles. After the first semester of our freshman year, he was in every class Miles took. He had a part-time job in the registrar's office. By the time I came along, I told Miles, "Surely you know this is not coincidental that the two of you both have the same major. He's stalking you!"

"Oh, surely not," Miles responded.

"All he has to do is look at your schedule and then align all his sections to match yours. That job of his is mighty convenient, it seems to me."

"Oh my god—I'd not thought about that!" Miles exclaimed.

I added, "He obviously can't carry a tune or he'd be in choir both at the college and Park Place—you see him sitting in the front rows every Sunday!"

Miles chuckled at that realization of this piece of the puzzle and said, "Heart-breaker Bergeron at it again."

Of course the guy tried whenever possible to sit next to Miles in class. I told Miles, "If your star status ever spawns a biography, he can write it. He probably has detailed records of the color socks you wore on any given day, what kind of pen you used to take notes and the brand of mechanical pencil you use in accounting classes."

"I'd hope it's not that bad," Miles said, "but it wouldn't surprise me either."

Our junior year, a sophomore transferred in who was a foreign student from the Middle East. I'd heard about him from Miles long before I'd ever seen him. The first word Miles used to describe him was "exotic." As described to me by Miles, he had a perfect dark-skin complexion, big black eyes, black silky hair and a "soccer player's build." Miles happened to sit out a production that fall which this new student happened to be in. Miles and I were sitting together in the auditorium, and when the young man first came onstage I let out a lipped-sealed but audible, "Uuummm!"

Miles jabbed me with his elbow, sure that everyone around us heard me—which they probably did, and knew why I'd made such a noise—which they probably didn't. I figured any who had clued in were thinking the same thing themselves. Even a straight man had to be taken aback. He *was* exotic.

By the spring term, suddenly the stalker vanished from Miles' classes. When Miles saw him one day down at the mailboxes in Decker Hall, he asked his stalker friend where he'd been.

"Oh, I changed my major," he said.

He had changed his major to the same as our exotic arrival, and he now had a new muse.

I asked Miles, "How does it feel to be traded in for a newer model?"

Miles said, "For the sake of him ever actually graduating, let's hope another infatuation doesn't come along in two years. He might never get out of here if he has to keep changing majors."

We both laughed, and I said, "Since my brother flunked out of college, Dad gave me some advice for getting my degree saying, 'Take what time you need but don't see how long you can take.' Maybe next time you see him you should give him that advice."

Miles' sympathetic nature returned, "He's a nice kid. Let's just hope he can find a way beyond his obsessions to actually be loved in return."

Chapter Twenty-one

Since my Torino held six while most of my friends' cars—if they had one—only seated four, I by default became the official driver to all outings. I didn't mind in those days. I still loved to drive—something I'd gotten over by the time I retired. We frequently went down to the circle in downtown Indianapolis on Friday nights just to do it. We would always eat somewhere too. Our little group of six included Miles, of course. One of the group finally talked me into going to White Castle for hamburgers. I couldn't believe my eyes! I'd heard about them but never eaten at one. Our go-to place while in Indianapolis was either Chi-Chi's or Steak 'n Shake. Here we were finally trying her "wonderful" White Castle burgers. I'm sorry—this old farm boy knows what a hamburger is, and a little square patty with holes in it ain't it! That city girl would often persuade the other crowd she ran with to go there, but that was the one and only time I ever went.

On more adventurous outings we'd take off for long weekends or over spring break when I could get away from work. One time we went to Chicago—in the days well before going online to find hotels or motels—and got there late at night.

We finally saw a motel and pulled in. I knew it couldn't be a good sign when the desk clerk inquired, "By the hour or by the night?"

If it weren't so late and we had any better idea where to go in town, we would have done so. As it was I reported back to him, "For the night."

Have mercy! There were phone numbers written all over the vinyl curtains and there was no way any of us were going to take off our clothes and get in those sheets! We got enough sleep, fully clothed, to rest up for the next day—which technically it already was. The funny thing about that trip and life's adventures is that it's the only thing I remember about our trip to Chicago! I don't remember what we did while there, or if we stayed a second night at a respectable motel or went back to Anderson.

The best trip was one spring break we drove to New Orleans. Fortunately on this adventure, we had Miles' familiarity with the city his having been there many times since Franklin, where Miles was from, is just a couple hours to the West. This time we had an affordable hotel room right down in the French Quarter with clean sheets and an indoor pool. We went up and down Royal and Bourbon and had café au lait and beignets every morning at Café du Monde. We spent most of one evening listening to Dixieland Jazz at Preservation Hall. A couple of days we went to the cemeteries in town—something Miles and I made a habit of all our years in all our travels—and walked around looking at names and the unique above-ground marble structures. One night we strolled past the brighter lights of Bourbon Street getting into what, to me, looked like pretty seedy surroundings. One of our friends—the lover of White Castle—said, "See those guys going in there? That looks like a gay bar. Let's go in."

She'd never been in any gay bar nor had any of the rest of us. I thwarted the idea with, "We might go in. I'm not sure we'd come back out." Since she was the only one who thought that was a good idea, we turned to "walk to the light" and back to our hotel.

I did love the food and was in no hurry to leave. I had my first muffulettas—at least three times for lunch. We feasted on gumbo and étouffée and Oysters Rockefeller. Miles, the crab lover, announced before we ever got there that he was going to have his favorite—Crab Imperial—which he did twice on the trip. He also knew of some seafood dive out toward Franklin not far from Oak Alley Plantation which we drove out to see on his recommendation. It is one of those markets where they dump crab and boiled shrimp out on newsprint and you dig in. We did, and that Cajun was still pickin' crab when the rest of us were long finished. There is no point in rushin' a Cajun eatin' crab! His final benediction was always the same for all his crab feasts, "Ç'est bon!"

Our little coterie of six also went to a couple of musical outings —one at Butler University and the other at IU in Bloomington. The first was a simple evening outing and the second an overnight trip.

Butler did a production of Leonard Bernstein's *Mass*. I can say two things about it. I'd never seen anything like it, and no Mennonite pastor would ever imagine it in their church. But it was powerful, amazing, and made me "ponder anew what the Almighty can do." I'm not sure the song that sticks with me most strongly to this day, *God Said*, is perhaps the best takeaway from it, but it is undeniable in its unvarnished truth. I'm pretty sure Bernstein would have gotten a good ear boxing if Grandma Shudel were his grandmother. It has a number of verses but there are a few which stuck in my mind. Each verse sets up a different premise of how we twist things to fit what we want as to what God said—it's good to be poor, so if we steal from you it's just to help you stay pure; we're in charge of the zoo, so what does it matter if we wipe out a species or two; God made us boss, gave us the cross and we turned it into a sword to spread the word of the Lord. As it sums it all up, we took what was "good" and made it "goddam good."

I can't quite hear *God Said* in four-part a cappella at Hope Mennonite, but I also have never gotten it out of my head. On the drive back to Anderson, we all just sat in the car speechless. I can't imagine coming out of a production of that magnitude any other way. I quickly ordered the sound track and even played it for Mom when I was home. I'm not sure she ever heard that last line of *God Said*, but she did think *Mass* was a powerful work. I didn't think Dad, being more inclined to cowboy songs, would find it something he would want to sit down and listen to. That Mom never suggested he do so, seemed to confirm she thought the same.

Our Bloomington adventure was to attend their production of *Porgy and Bess*. Holy moly! When that curtain first came up and I saw that set, this old carpenter and set builder was blown away. As one would expect with IU's musical renown, the singing was incredible. It certainly didn't have the impact *Mass* had on me, but I can still see that stage set.

Miles and I used to drive over to Muncie for nothing in particular. One time, we went just to take black-and-white photos of "urban blight"—not that we had to leave Anderson to do that. The notorious teamster, Jimmy Hoffa, went missing about the time we entered Anderson. On the drive between Anderson and Muncie there was an old garage—no house around—where an old, wrecked car had driven into the now-wrecked garage. Miles would always say, "I still think we need to stop and see if Jimmy Hoffa's in that car. They've been looking for him all this time."

We never did stop to see, and they never did find poor Jimmy. Could be he's still there—just bones and his crumbling leather wallet left.

Chapter Twenty-two

Miles arrived on campus with a red Triumph Spitfire convertible which was cute as heck and fun to drive. I liked his car even before I liked him! It wasn't all that practical though, in the gray, cold months in central Indiana. You certainly had to be sure the battery was good because it would take forever to start in cold weather and some days just refused. The rest of the year it was great. It wasn't the safest car. The 1968 model didn't have any seat belts, and Miles said if it ever looked like he was going to have an encounter with a semi, he would steer towards the trailer, duck and hope he came out the other side with only the windshield torn off. Fortunately, we never had even a little fender bender in that car. Whenever we wanted to go somewhere and ensure we didn't pick up any who might want to tag along, we'd be sure to take the Spitfire. As a two-seater, there was no way for anyone else to ride along.

One weekend at the end of our junior year, we got a two-man tent and a Coleman stove and lantern and headed down to Brown County State Park for a few days break before the weather got any hotter. We had the Spitfire top down all the way going and coming and were fortunate enough to have perfect weather. However, we did venture onto a trail without fully knowing what we'd given ourselves over to.

After an hour of walking, Miles said, "We have been going down hill all this time."

I said, "I've thought about turning around, but surely we have got to be nearing the low point and hopefully the grade back up will have at least a few flatter areas to recover."

If it did I don't remember it. It seemed like it was twice as far back up as it was down.

Miles had added a stereo tape player to the Triumph and, while we'd cook out each evening, he'd turn on a couple of his favorites he brought along—Barber's *Adagio for Strings* and Vivaldi's *Four Seasons*. Both seemed fitting music to reflect on as we made our home those few days deep in the woods of Brown County.

I told him, "Too bad we didn't bring a tape of the Park Place choir and that Casavant organ so we could play Beethoven's

Hallelujah real loud on Sunday morning and wake up all the heathens."

Miles said, "We might rather behave since I think we may want to come back here every now and then." He added, "You could even give up that idea of yours of going to LSU and apply to IU. Then we could come out here anytime we wanted."

I wasn't quite ready to give up on my romantic notion of what it would be like to be in the deep south with all that good Cajun cooking, and just said, "I guess I could think about it"—which I never really did. I figured my academic standing already would be hard enough at LSU, and I had a notion it was a lost cause at IU. Who knows if that was true, in fact, or a construct only in my mind. Regardless, it prevailed in my thoughts, and I never applied.

Saturday night in the two-man tent, I shared with Miles for the first time the story of my night in the pup tent with Wesley. While that night was never far from my thoughts, I'd never shared it with anyone and found, as I did so, that I couldn't hold back the emotion of its history. I began to cry.

Miles was shocked. "I didn't think Swiss Mennonites had tear ducts."

It wasn't said in the tone of the humor both of us were always more inclined towards. He could always mourn with those who mourn, and as he said those words, he was crying for me or Wesley or every boy and girl who sob in the night for whatever fears and troubles are in their lives. At which point, we still didn't know of the abuse that had plagued Wesley and his mother and his sisters.

When the heaviness of the moment passed, Miles said, "I always knew, somehow, I wasn't the first boy you loved even though you said I was. If that township school hadn't split, and you and Wesley had graduated with each other, I bet the two of you would have figured out some way to go off and be together."

"Perhaps that might have happened," I said. "It might have even happened if I had just pulled his arm into mine that night in a gentle embrace. I wonder if he's ever imagined his life with such a possibility. I wonder if he still weeps at night for what might have been had I just known what to do for him in that moment. That might have been his one time to risk opening up to another, and I failed him. Perhaps he never felt safe enough with anyone else to ever try."

We were both silent for a time, then I added, "But to set the record straight once and for all, he wasn't the first and you weren't the second. Beany was my first love."

"Beany?" Miles asked.

I explained. "Don't you remember the cartoon *Beany and Cecil*? Beany had that long blond hair, blue eyes and a little propellor on his cap?"

"Vaguely," he answered.

"I must have only been about five when that first came on TV, and when we went to a department store Christmas shopping, they had 'Beany' dolls. Next time we're at Mom and Dad's, I'll introduce you. She still has him in the chest with the toys for the grandkids. I don't know if this is significant on my Mom's part or not, but it's the only doll in the treasure trove of toys. Anyway, when I saw Beany in the store I said I wanted it, and when it looked liked I wasn't going to get him, I remember holding Mom's hand as we went on with the shopping with me crying the whole time—all the way out to the car and, broken-hearted the whole way home. Christmas Eve when we opened gifts, there was Beany—the best Christmas present ever! The propeller soon broke off because Beany slept in my bed every night and you know how I roll around.

"So for the record, you were my third—two cute blonds and now a black-haired Cajun."

He thought he had a good comeback to that. "I lost track of where you line up. Probably seventh or eighth at least."

I said straightforwardly, "I've known it all along."

Sunday morning before heading back to Anderson, we decided to take the Spitfire for a drive rather than stumble onto another never-ending uphill trail. We stopped by Ogle Lake. We saw another young man with a golden retriever puppy—all legs and not much meat on his bones at that point. When the dog saw that water, he was off in a flash—leash and all. Hauling-ass, he leapt from the bank about ten feet into the water and paddled around until finally he came back on shore, shook off, picked up his own leash and came back to his master. We were standing next to the young man by then watching the free entertainment. He told us while the dog was swimming that he'd just recently gotten him and this was the first he knew of that the dog had been in water.

"What an instinct," I said.

That dog was so fun to watch in the water and walking around with his own leash, when we got back in the Triumph Miles said, "We gotta get one of those one of these days." It would be a long time, but we would get not one but two, and then two more after that.

Chapter Twenty-three

I lived in an upstairs apartment from my sophomore year on, and Miles joined me there our last two years in Anderson. I had to show that I could live cheaper off campus than on, which didn't take much doing. My apartment was furnished and included the utilities. I kept the place pretty freezing in the winter since I was used to a cold house and an even colder bedroom. I thought the Cajun would crank up the heat and run up my rent, but he liked it cold. I think the landlord probably noticed how low the utility bills were once I moved in and appreciated the fact that I always paid my rent early, so in all three years he never raised the rent. It was already half of what I would have paid in most places for a smaller apartment.

We did have colorful neighbors downstairs. Sadly, both were alcoholics. They each lived in separate one-bedroom apartments that had been carved out of the old house. I had the entire upstairs with its two bedrooms. They would drink together, it seemed like almost every evening. She would get louder and louder the drunker she got. Miles and I both found her colorful language somewhat amusing even as we pitied their drunken state of being. Both were always kind to us, and we were always kind to them. Every once in a while, I would take them cinnamon rolls or sugar cookies I'd made from Mom's recipes.

When the drinking would start, which always took place in his apartment right under our living room, he would say something that we could never quite make out. She would holler back at him, "Don't give me any of that ssshhhiiittt!"

I'll bet we heard that line a hundred times—probably more.

One spring morning our senior year, Miles said, "There's an ambulance out front."

We went down to see, just as they rolled the old lady out of her apartment. She had died and her old drinking buddy was standing outside crying. He said, "What am I going to do with that cat? She loved that cat and that cat loved her."

We knew exactly what he was going to do with that big, old, fat tabby cat. It would be spending the rest of its days with him as long as he or the cat lasted.

Miles and I added two lines to our own colloquial sayings that we'd never forget.

"Don't give me any of that ssshhhiiittt!" As we'd say it, we would roll out our bottom lip as far as possible—as we'd pictured this was how she drew out that word ssshhhiiittt!

And the other line, of course. "She loved that cat and that cat loved her."

It was amazing just how many ways we found to fit those into conversations over the years.

I had quite a life in college, most of which wasn't in the classroom. Nor was it hugging a toilet after another night of binge drinking or having countless one-night stands one soon forgets or regrets. Still, you can see the problem—the inherent fault of my academic pursuits. I did know how to have a good time and can recall, with a good deal of joy and gratitude, all our adventures. I just never could find even one semester of consistency across my classes where joy, gratitude and enthusiasm would be words I could draw upon to describe it. Maybe that's true for everyone in academia—but I certainly hope, for the professors at least, such is not the case. As much as some bored me, I'm afraid it might have be more the norm than the exception. But judge not! At any rate, I'll always take learning by experience over learning by textbook— any time.

Our sophomore year, the college brought in a minister from another state as the speaker for a week of special services. This was an annual event in which, in addition to the twice-weekly chapel services, every evening there would be another service where the guest speaker would preach. These even preempted evening classes for that week so I was able to always attend.

Miles filled me in on his first appearance at chapel that Tuesday morning. "He has kind of a southern drawl, and when he started out I thought, 'this is going to be a long week.' He spoke rather slowly and without much inflection, but somewhere, about ten minutes in, I found myself tuned-in like I rarely ever have been during a sermon. Certainly not any of those homilies back in Franklin."

I looked forward to my first opportunity to hear this guy firsthand at the Wednesday evening service. Miles was right—he didn't look impressive or sound impressive at first, but it didn't take long for me to become intrigued with his weaving of poetry into his preaching. Whatever notes he might have had in front of him, it was clear the poems were from memory. Every sermon that week included many such poetic inclusions that definitely spilled over into his own poetic style of storytelling.

On the last Sunday night of the services, he shared with us his own personal story. He was a poor student academically who never expected to get into college—in fact his high school guidance counselor told him to consider a trade as he'd never get accepted. His determined mother had other ideas. She persuaded their local college to give him a chance which they did. He was getting along mostly except for his most dreaded subject—English. There he wasn't going to make it. To his good fortune, he had a professor who ventured to ask herself how she might help this boy. She risked moving beyond the boundaries of the conformity within the curriculum when she noticed that, anytime a poem came up in some context of the class, he seemed to awaken. One day after class she asked him to stay.

"Clement, you aren't going to make it in this class the way things are going now—I know you know that. I have a proposition for you. Here is a collection of poems by many different poets. If you will memorize a new poem for every session, then I will pass you in this class."

She was a rule breaker, and it worked. What he couldn't straighten in his mind on sentence structure and grammar he could record in that mind of his—every word of the poets he learned to love. Her singular intervention in his life layered on top of his mother, who insisted her boy be given a chance, changed Clement's life and planted the seeds for the pastoral life he used to feed so many.

It is no exaggeration to say that good man unlocked that corner of my own mind and what had been my mind's resistance to "academic pursuits." I began to awaken to poets whose poetry told stories—Frost's *Death of the Hired Man*, *The Witch of Coos*, and *Birches*; Muir's *The Good Town* and *The Horses*; Kipling's *Eddi's*

Service; and in later years, just about every poem ever written by Wendell Berry—who I would latch onto as an old farm boy with particular affection. I never would be a fan of what I would call "intellectual poetry"—that is where, it seems to me, the poets give all their energy in trying be both esoteric and clever. It always appeared to me they were most interested in impressing themselves with themselves. I'm sure this is as much about my own shortcomings—at least it *must* be—since the ones I can't relate to in any form or fashion seem to always win awards.

Giving credit where credit is due, Miles' and my overall experience in Anderson, both at the college and Park Place, were very good times in our lives and molded us as much as anything "to think anew and act anew," to borrow Mr. Lincoln's famous line. And we would find ourselves molded to our alma mater song— even with its now gender-specific (offensive to some) language.

Anderson our alma mater
Guide of soul and mind.
Thou hast taught within thy borders
to aid all mankind.

So, for this thy noble purpose
may our best avail.
Friend of all that's good and upright,
Hail to thee! All hail.

Chapter Twenty-four

My parents and Miles' dad had all shown up for our graduation in June. I would have been glad to skip the ceremony altogether, but unlike my ability to keep my singing of the *National Anthem* from my parents, they knew graduation was coming and were not going to let me get away with skipping the ceremony. It meant nothing to me for some reason. I borrowed the cap and gown from a graduate the year before so the year on the band of the tassel was 1978 instead of 1979. About all I remember of the ceremony is the senator who stood there making a long speech on something about his agriculture policies.

His peculiar topic of choice wasn't lost on Dad who said right afterwards, "What the Sam Hill did that speech have to do with students graduating from Anderson?"

The highlight of this last trip to Anderson for them was Sunday morning at Park Place which both always enjoyed—Mom for the music followed by the preaching, and Dad for the preaching followed by the music. This was the first time Miles' dad came to the campus and so his first time at Park Place as well. We were asked to sing one of our duets and we did our most rousing piece— the arrangement by Ovid Young of *Jesus Paid It All*—made popular by the duo Hale and Wilder.

Miles' dad sat with my folks and all three were about a third of the way back in the Sanctuary, straight out from the lectern where we stood to sing. In those days, we rarely if ever applauded in church. Some churches would. Hope Mennonite and Park Place did not. I approved of this and wish it was still more the norm than the exception. It was certainly enough for us to know we'd sung our hearts out, and it was clear enough our parents were mesmerized by our harmony together.

Two rows in front of our parents was a very familiar, friendly face, my gentle dean. Right after the service he approached me as I headed down the side aisle to where they were. He was a regular at Park Place and one who I had forged an unexpected connection with.

I was beginning to struggle towards the end of my senior year and began to wonder if I would graduate. I have no idea how he knew that. I hadn't even talked to Miles about how down I was. I'm a master at covering emotion—or at least I thought I was. Something must have clued in the gentle dean. I've always had some melancholy dog me, but this was closer to real depression— inexplicable but real. One day he called and said he wanted to see me. You would think that meant a trip to his office in Decker Hall, but no, he was coming to me. He was going to help me be sure I got through to graduation, but somehow he knew that wasn't the root of the problem. Like many of the administrators, he was also an ordained minister and had his doctorate. After talking about the courses I was in and might need help with in some form or fashion he was quick to transition. It should be noted he was very near retiring and past when he could have retired.

"August, whenever you lead the music on Sunday night, or sing a solo, or a duet with Miles, you see me there, and I always come up to you afterwards to thank you."

"Yes, I know you do. It's very kind," I replied.

He continued, "I don't go to church on Sunday night because I need to hear another sermon. I've heard all I ever need to and then some. I don't go if some out-of-town group is coming in 'to perform.' I go for one reason, and that is, to be there to support you."

I began to cry. Why did this gentle man have any heart of compassion for me? And how was it, he was here at my lowest point lifting me back up on my feet? He seemed to have uncovered the root of my angst which I had not been able to see myself until then. I said to him through those tears, "Everybody seems to know what God is calling them to do, and I don't have a clue even though I pray about it all the time. People go off to 'do ministry.' They talk about the family they are going to have. The career they are going to have. I have no idea what I'm doing."

He put one hand gently on my knee as we sat facing each other, "You are giving old men like me hope, and when the old have hope from the young, then we can pass from this life with more hope still for those who follow. I don't know if that makes any sense to you, but the only 'calling' is to be yourself and live a life of gratitude for each and every gift you have and each and every soul who touches yours. You can leave Anderson knowing you've touched souls—

this old man's and others I know. In life, we can't know which souls we will touch—or how deeply—and that's okay. But you will touch others' lives and they will touch yours. My dear, August, that's all you really need. Everyone's vocation is to love God, love yourself and love your neighbor. Some people confuse vocation with job success and these are *not* the same. *Let them* be sure. If you find doubts as one of your companions along your journey, then you know one old man who said, 'give your doubts consideration—pondering is a good thing.'"

His recitation of the "Hope Mennonite creed" made my tears give way to a bit of a smile. A good many preachers would have ended with a prayer. He seemed to know pious words weren't needed. He'd said enough. He stood and, putting his right hand out, held my right hand with both his hands for a moment and left. That was the one and only real conversation we ever had and one that has never left me.

As I smiled brightly at the gentle dean here on this last Sunday at Park Place, Mom, Dad and Miles' dad, Frankie (Francois), approached. I'd never said anything to anyone about my conversation those weeks earlier with the gentle dean. I just introduced him to my parents, first by name and title, but quickly added, "This kind man changes insecure students from a fumbling mess to what they might hope to become."

My dad reached out to shake his hand with a big smile and said, "If you can do that, I can't imagine there is a higher calling for anyone on earth."

The gentle dean said back to my dad, "In August's case, it seemed to me all the heavy-duty work was already done back home. I just had to remind him such was the case."

I, the non-hugger, wanted to give him a big hug right then, and he must have known it. He hugged me, and made me cry again like I did that day of his timely intervention in my life.

Dad got back to our singing and lightened the mood. "You always fussed about those voice lessons you said we *made* you take. It looked to me like there wasn't anything in the world you wanted to do more just then than sing."

I had a pretty good response to that, I thought. "You never saw me that happy singing a solo did you? I always liked to sing.

Taking lessons, you were supposed to like to sing alone, and I never have and doubt I ever will!"

All these exchanges mildly perplexed Frankie. I'm sure he was ready for Miles to make his way to us. Where he was, I didn't know. Someone had snagged him somewhere. Our exchange humored my mother. She and I were humored easily, sometimes so much so Dad couldn't figure out what was so funny though he knew often enough it was us laughing at his more serious nature. This was a "gift" she and I shared in common that my siblings never did. They all tended to the more serious.

It never took much for us to be humored. We'd be giggling at the dinner table and he'd say, "You two are crazy!"

All Mom said of the duet was, "Your grandparents sure would've liked to have heard that." And then to Miles, who had finally shown up, she said, "You better keep this boy singing with you when you get to Louisiana."

As we were preparing to leave the church, Dad said to me, "Don't forget where you've come from."

Mom added, "And don't forget to look where you're going."

And the gentle dean smiled saying, "Well, that pretty well sums it up, doesn't it, August?"

Their words sounded so simple then—almost trite—but as I would reflect on them in different times of my life, they were indeed for me seeds of contemplation. I might have written a book entitled that someday, *Seeds of Contemplation*. Merton beat me to it.

Union, Justice, and Confidence

Chapter Twenty-five

After our final Sunday at Park Place, Miles' dad was loaded and ready to go. He headed home straight from the church. My mom and dad had stayed at our apartment, and we went back to have a quick lunch, pack up the last little bit we needed to put in our cars and hit the road. Since our apartment in Anderson was furnished, we had no need for a U-Haul for the little bit we had. As I'd moved there four years earlier loading up Mom and Dad's Bonneville, now the only notable change was the man I was moving with.

Our plan to drive straight through to Louisiana came to an unexpected obstacle. I was in my Torino hauling most all our clothes, books and personal items. Miles was following behind in the Spitfire with it loaded up as well. As the time approached midnight, we were driving through northern Mississippi when I noticed in my rearview mirror that the headlights on the Spitfire were getting dimmer and dimmer. Something was wrong. I pulled off the next exit, which was in the middle of nowhere, with no services and pitch dark. By the time we pulled off on the berm of the service road the old girl died—the battery too dead to start the car. We didn't want to abandon the car though we seriously considered it.

It was a hot and sticky night and the mosquitos weren't terrible but were bad enough. We decided about all we could do was wait for daylight and then go try to find help at another exit further down the road. Neither one of us could recall anything nearby over the road we'd already covered. All we could do was press on.

As though we weren't already tense about the situation, it didn't help that within ten minutes of our stopping, two jacked-up pickups with big spotlights over the cabs and straight-pipes to make them as loud as possible came down the service road. As they passed us, they deliberately gunned it, peeling rubber and throwing beer cans out the window at us. We were both sure that was just their warm-up act, and they would soon be back to kick the shit out of us. We were both in the Torino ready to leave if we saw their lights coming back our way. Thank God, they didn't come back, and we didn't see another car or truck all night. But it was a hot, sticky, miserable night, and with fear of what might come along, neither of us got anything approaching a restful night.

At first dawn, Miles went back to the Spitfire and gave it a try to see if it would start. The battery had come back to life just enough to start the car, and we got back on the road. At the next exit there was a garage. It was bigger than the standard service station but smaller than a full-blown truck stop. The half-toothed mechanic, cigarette hanging out one side of his mouth as he talked out the other side, offered to take a look. It didn't take him five minutes to diagnose the problem.

He said, "The alternator's dead."

We didn't have to ask if they happened to stock 1968 Triumph Spitfire parts. We explained where we'd come from and where we were headed. We knew we were shit out of luck and just had to decide how we were going to deal with it. Do we leave it with them, scrounge up the needed alternator from somewhere, sometime and come back, or do we just give up the car and call it a day? Miles had only paid $500 for it when he bought it. It's not like we had a whole lot to lose leaving it there for good. We did think it would be hard to get Miles and what was in the Spitfire crammed into the Torino, but thought that might be the only option. Then the mechanic, who had disappeared for a moment, was back.

He said, "I went to check something out in the back of the yard. The owner has his own mini-junkyard back there, and I knew there was one old Triumph among the cars. It's a different model, but I checked and the alternator is the same. I called the owner and he said, 'If it works, they can have it. Just charge 'em for the labor.' If that sounds good to you, I'll go pull it and we'll see."

I said, "That would be great."

He was off to get the alternator and Miles and I stared at each other in complete disbelief. It took the mechanic all of ten minutes to put it in.

He said to Miles, "See if it cranks."

She started right up and was charging the battery. He had Miles turn the lights on and they didn't dim a bit. It was working just fine.

"What do we owe?" I asked.

He responded, "Oh, how's twenty-five sound?"

I got out my wallet and handed him two twenties. I said, "Forty sounds better. Please thank the owner for us. You both have been real lifesavers."

His parting words were, "If you were going to break down, you certainly picked the right spot. That old Triumph has sat out there totaled for years. You must be livin' right. You boys have a safe trip."

The gentle dean had done more than get me out of my depression and ensure I graduated. He had also called his counterpart at LSU and made arrangements for me to take one "leveling" class in the summer to get me accepted into their MBA program. My final GPA was technically point-one percent too low. The gentle dean, checking with my professors that final term, knew it was going to come out that way and persuaded the dean at LSU that I deserved the chance. I didn't have time to dawdle. With our nighttime Mississippi adventure we were running about eight hours behind our planned time, and the first session of the summer class I was taking started at 5:30 PM. It left me plenty of time to get to the admissions office to check in, to the bookstore to get my favorite thing—another expensive textbook—and to my class, but I was so tired I'm sure the professor thought I looked like something the cat drug in.

For Miles, Louisiana was a going-home, whether he wanted to or not. He had been close to his mother, Bella (Savoie), and not so much with his father, but she was dead from breast cancer by the end of his freshman year. He flew home for Christmas that year and she was gone by Easter. We didn't know each other then, so I didn't know how hard that freshman year might have been for him.

By the time we talked about it, all he really said was, "Her last words to me were, 'Don't wallow in grief. Live your life. It passes too quickly to spend it in sorrow.'" He certainly did try to honor her request.

Clearly, if I'd been a better student, I'd have done more homework on Louisiana before moving him back there.

Ohio didn't have a pledge of allegiance, per se. And Mennonites are not pledge takers. If it starts with, "I pledge allegiance to," we've got a problem. It doesn't even take any particular cherry-picking of verses in the Bible to see where that might present a problem—though many a Christian easily enough ignores it. We did have our 4-H pledge, which didn't present itself as a problem for me or any of our extended family who was so actively involved all those years with 4-H.

I pledge my head to clearer thinking,
My heart to greater loyalty,
My hands to larger service,
and my health to better living,
for my club, my community, my country, and my world.

Shoot, you could say that and still follow the Hope Mennonite creed without an iota of contradiction.

Hopefully it doesn't take a genius, unfamiliar with 4-H, to see the four Hs are—head, heart, hands and health. Simple as that pledge is, as my years progressed I never had any trouble finding room for improvement across the board.

Two years after we arrived, Louisiana adopted—or updated, I'm not sure which—their pledge of allegiance. Louisiana did not improve on the 4-H pledge.

I pledge allegiance to the flag of the state of Louisiana and to the motto for which it stands: A state, under God, united in purpose and ideals, confident that justice shall prevail for all of those abiding here.

I'd already learned the hard way what Miles thought of the state motto, *Union, Justice and Confidence*, when we first moved there. I had to admit too, I was in a place where that motto didn't align at all with what I knew about the history and practice up to our day of southern justice. Not that I had a perfected notion of northern justice—but lynchings, segregation and poverty were foreign to my world. I wondered if I'd wandered into a culture of denial that would trouble me more than I was willing to deal with for very long.

I said, "Can you tell me the state motto?"

"No," he said. "I never took Louisiana history."

I didn't think you needed a class to know the state motto, but I didn't say anything. I recited the motto to him.

He had a visceral reaction. "What a bunch of *bullshit!*"

I had gotten Miles wound up without intending to do so. Clearly agitated he said, "My black grade school pal, Tommy Lee, whose daddy was lynched and burned up, can tell you all about their unity and justice. No one ever knew why they even singled him out. As best we could tell, he happened to be in the wrong place at the wrong time—and the wrong place is anywhere those *bastards* decide it's the wrong place. Tommy Lee's mother was a nervous wreck with Tommy Lee and me even being friends. She was afraid of what that could mean for Tommy Lee playing with a white boy—and that was even before his daddy was lynched and burned."

Holy shit! I didn't even know he had a black friend in grade school, or that he ever knew anyone who had such a gruesome and unjust death. I was quickly learning that coming back here was going to open wounds he'd tucked away while in our more blissful days in Anderson.

I said back to him, "I had no idea! You've never said anything to me about that before."

He said, just as sharply as he'd recounted the horrors of Tommy Lee's father, "Welcome to Louisiana. And yes when I was born, whites still had their fountains and blacks had theirs; whites had their restrooms and blacks had theirs; whites sat downstairs at the movies and blacks up in the balcony; whites had their schools and blacks had theirs. The welcome mat wasn't rolled out at the universities either. It is some better now as long as you don't look too close, but that motto is total *bullshit!*"

I realized I'd peeled off an old scab from a wound that had not healed after all these years. I wasn't sure which of his recitations of the way things were pertained to Franklin or just Louisiana in general, or maybe the whole Deep South. As I would learn, the courts finally ordered "full integration" of LSU in 1964—though as with most integration rulings, there was no rush to admit Blacks en masse. I wondered how many other revelations I might stumble

104

upon exposing other old wounds. For now I'd let the Cajun, who I'd come to know better over the next five years as my "ragin' Cajun," be for the time being.

Chapter Twenty-six

I got busy looking for a job, and Miles started his. We stayed in a cheap motel two nights before finding a hole-in-the-wall apartment close to the university. Miles had majored in accounting and computer science in college and had applied to both departments at LSU before we moved. He had no problem getting a job in the administrative computing department. His hedged-bet of a double-major strategy paid off, as they were delighted to have someone with an accounting degree they could assign to the finance division.

My management degree didn't yield any immediate prospects at the university. I knew a BA in Business was a dime-a-dozen major which is the only reason I was going on for an MBA. It certainly wasn't my love of getting degrees. We figured universities were more likely not to get too nosy over our personal lives or at least do anything about it, while working for businesses in town might lead to getting fired when they put two and two together. Whether this was an accurate reading of our options or not is hard to say. It seemed real enough and probably was.

Before leaving Anderson I had decided I might need to fall back on my construction skills and look in that direction if the university didn't have anything that looked like a fit for me. I quickly found a contractor who liked the combination of my management degree and practical experience. He hired me to project-manage his bigger jobs.

By the end of June we were both getting a paycheck; and I was plodding through my one required, leveling class and was registered for the fall term to begin my MBA.

It was good we had those Anderson years to ease into our relationship. What followed in Baton Rouge would be the hardest five years of our life together.

Away from Anderson and back down in the Old South, Miles took up a bad habit he'd had in high school—smoking. I couldn't stand it! We were already dealing with the tension of his new job and my school and working at a job out in the heat. My mood was bad and his was worse. One time when we'd just bought two white cotton long sleeve shirts, he got out the ironing board and iron and started to press them. I'd never seen the likes of it. He was attacking the shirt and not ironing it. He managed to rip a hole in the first one and ruined it—which only made him all the madder. I took the iron away from him before he ruined the other one.

What drove me craziest of all was getting up and showering in the morning, as I would smell that first cigarette wafting into the bathroom of our small apartment. It made for a grumpy start to my day—every day. I did draw the line on smoking in the car. I didn't care how long the drive—he had to wait to smoke until we would stop.

The smoking went on the entire time we lived in Baton Rouge. Whether coincidental or not, his teeth started to go bad and we'd no sooner landed in Boone when he had the dentist pull all of them out. His parents both had dentures as did his older brothers—all of whom smoked—so parting with teeth early on seemed to be a family trait.

Smoking was not something I ever took up—though I suppose gluttony was no virtue, and we both liked to eat. He was crab crazy. I loved fried catfish, hush puppies and coleslaw. My mother made a wonderful vinegar-based slaw which I missed (and would make on occasion), but in the South it was all cream-based. I liked it too and had for some time. When I was in Anderson, and friends wanted to go to Perkins late at night and pig out, I couldn't afford to buy a meal so I always ordered coleslaw and water. I always liked slaw with any fried foods—catfish, shrimp, cod, chicken. Still do for that matter. I just don't eat any of those breaded or battered foods anymore. Now I'm back to meals where I just have slaw or cottage cheese and water. Not because of finances as it was in college—they just sound good sometimes, and it's all I need these days.

Chapter Twenty-seven

Oh, lord—that first summer in the heat working outside full time, I thought I'd died and gone to hell. All I could think about was the shade and relative cool of Brown County. I still wanted to like the South and hoped that I would acclimate. I told myself since we landed in summer—what did I expect? I hadn't given myself any chance to ease into it. Fall would be here soon enough, and by next summer, I'd feel like I lived here all my life. I couldn't complain about the company I worked for. Summer being their busiest time afforded me full-time work in the summers, and they let me flex my hours during the school year averaging around 30 hours a week—some weeks as few as 20 but rarely.

In those days I noticed how quickly I adapted to dialects in the South. I could instantly fit in without sounding like the upper midwesterner I really was. I wasn't trying to be clever about it. To me, it was natural and seemed respectful. I would never have a deep drawl like some do, but they never mistook me for the "Yankee" they had disdain for most of the time. It didn't take me long to see how they came to feel that way about Yanks either. One of our clients was from New York originally, and I'd never experienced the condescension he thought was his right to impose on those hired to do his bidding. He just assumed I was native and was as bad to me as he was to the rest. It pleased me that such was the case and caught the eye of one of the black men on the crew, Louie, who pulled me aside after the Yank had reamed me out about something.

Louie said, "I've known that man a while. If he knew you was from up north he'd treat ya better. You might wanna drop a hint sometime."

I said, "Louie, I ain't no better than anyone else on this crew. And if he's hollering at me, it's all the less likely he'll have a chance, with his attention span, to holler at anybody else."

Louie already kinda liked me for reasons I couldn't articulate. He smiled at me and said, "August, you're a good man."

Of all the men on the crew, I was always closest to Louie and two other men he worked with all the time—CJ and Darnell. I can't remember anything about most of the others. There was one kid—I say kid, but he was older than me—who seemed prone to do the dumbest thing that could be done in any situation. He didn't last long, and I didn't have to get him fired—he just quit comin' to work.

Louie summed him up best, "Listenin' to good sense isn't a habit he ever picked up on."

Louie, CJ and Darnell were a good thirty years older than me. They did all the concrete forming, pouring and finishing, bringing in temp help or others from the framing side of the crew to help on big pours. Other help was rarely needed.

Louie heard some man making a pitch to me about how superior his concrete skills were to our crew.

After the man was gone, Louie said to me what I already knew. "August, you got a concrete man says his concrete don't crack, you got a liar for a concrete man."

I said, "Hire a braggart—get a bully. No thank you—don't want either one around here."

Louie was without a doubt the strongest man I ever knew. He was just over six feet tall and built like a brick shithouse. His biceps were enormous. His crew would also build retaining walls and when the customer wanted rail road ties, Louie could drive the twelve inch spikes we used to tie them down with three blows of his hammer. With every strike he would exhale an audible, "Huugh!" Driving the spike four inches with every blow. I stood in amazement every time.

He'd grown up in the country—quite a ways from town—and his daddy sold railroad ties to the railroad. He and his brothers felled the trees, cut them into ties and soaked them in creosote. (I had my own encounter with creosote one time as a teenager and looked like I'd been boiled alive—I assume they took more care than I knew to do.)

The three men would cut up as they worked. CJ would start off on some claim about this or that and Louie would come back with, "CJ, I've forgot more than you ever knew." They talked around me like I'd lived with them my whole life. You could see their speech and demeanor change in an instant anytime people they weren't comfortable with came around, including the owner of the company and a few of my white brethren on the crew—and always, whoever we were working for. They would move into what I can only think to call "their subservient persona" that they believed (and were probably all too correct in assuming) was expected of them. Everybody then was "yez-Miss" this and "yez-Mister" that—never even using the first names of the people they were responding to—always the surname. I hated it, and realized how blessed I was not to ever hear from them "Yeza, Mr. Kilber" or even "Yeza, Mr. August." To Louie, CJ and Darnell, I was always just August.

When I first heard Tyler, Johnny and Jimmy call me Mr. August, I was taken back to Louie, CJ and Darnell—and had the immediate and happy realization that when the boys called me "Mr. August," they said it out of simple respect for an old man and later with genuine affection. I thought, it's nice to see the next generations finding space to move beyond the expected subservience the generations before had to endure. I knew this was so much of the mettle of Momma Daisy and Pappy had worked into their lives.

For lunch we always ate on the job site. The three men always brought their lunch with them to work as did I in those days. I couldn't afford to eat out every day, and I suppose neither could they—or it was just a hold over from times when finding a restaurant to seat them was harder than not.

Louie had a gold plated front tooth with a diamond in it. It sparkled in the sun every time he would bare those teeth in a good laugh or big smile. He also carried a small New Testament with the Psalms in the upper pocket of the bib overalls he always wore. In the hot months, with one strap unhooked and no shirt on to allow a little air in. Every morning on his break, he would go off by himself and pull out that Bible and read. He never talked about what he'd read, and I never asked. I don't know if he just read straight through and started again at the beginning or if he had certain passages he'd read over and over according to the goings on at the time and his mood. I'd have been more inclined to the latter.

All three had plenty of stories about the black man's life in the white man's world. Darnell remained mostly a follower and could clearly validate Louie and CJ's accounts as like unto his own, but I don't recall him ever sharing a direct personal story about himself. I never knew about his family either—other than that he had a wife and grown kids. I knew plenty about the other two.

CJ had a wife and grown children in New Orleans, but he lived full-time in Baton Rouge. In Baton Rouge he had a lady friend, Gloria, who had her own house and family but no husband by then. It was no secret she spent plenty of nights over at CJ's. CJ wanted to know if I wanted to join them sometime for dinner at the buffet. He knew I had a "roommate" named Miles and said he should come too. Maybe because of their less-than-sanctioned arrangement, neither CJ nor Gloria seemed bothered by the notion of two grown men living together.

Miles looked at me rather peculiarly when I first announced the invitation but said, "I'd like to meet 'em. You talk so much about 'em."

The first buffet dinner together led to another and another. As long as we lived in Baton Rouge we went to dinner at least once a month and it felt like family of a kind.

CJ happened to retire the same time we moved to Boone. And he did, in fact, go back to New Orleans and pick up with his family as he always said he would. Gloria seemed to take it in stride— such was their peculiar arrangement. Though we lost touch after the two of us moved, I have little doubt that he made the drive to Baton Rouge at least once a month.

While Louie talked about his family, I never went to dinner with them. One day, Louie told me about a time he drove into a town in a parish north of where he lived. He stopped in front of the hardware store and got out to go in. As he was getting out of his pickup, a policeman pulled up, got out and said, "Boy, you can't park there." The "boy" was at least twice the age of the police "man" who gave him the order. Louie looked around and saw there wasn't a single sign, yellow curb or anything else to indicate he'd parked improperly. Regardless, without saying a word he got back in the truck, went past the downtown buildings and parked at the curb in front of the filling station next to the railroad tracks. Here was the cop again, "You can't park there, boy."

This time Louie said, "Where can I park?"

The answer came back with a point of the policeman's finger—"Across them tracks."

Louie said, "I drove across them tracks and never did park. I drove five miles out of my way on the way back home just not to have to drive back through that town again."

All I could do was stand there with my mouth half-open and shake my head, in what I would like to say was disbelief—when in fact it was the simple confirmation of what I knew to be their truth.

The worst day was when Louie arrived at work, and I could see right away something was wrong. I said to him, "What's wrong, Louie?"

"August, they shot my boy." he said.

"What?" I naturally exclaimed.

"Drive-by shooting—they shot my oldest. Killed him. He's got a wife and three kids. Now he's dead."

Well, if there is an appropriate response to that I certainly didn't know what it was supposed to be—still don't know all these years later. I knew what not to say—"he's in a better place." All that came out was, "Lord, have mercy."

I couldn't believe he'd come to work that morning and suggested he go back home. He did not. The day of the funeral was the only day he took off. It wasn't two weeks later he came to work in someone's borrowed truck.

"Where's your truck?" I asked.

"They stole my truck and all my tools."

I didn't know who "they" were and neither did Louie, but that man did not need such trouble upon trouble. A good many would have taken that little Bible he had and chucked it in the trash. Not Louie. Every morning break—there he would be off in a quiet place finding whatever solace the words brought him that the world refused to grant.

Chapter Twenty-eight

Miles in his new job was programming like a house afire. He was automating things the department hadn't even imagined possible with the punch cards that drove systems in those days. As the technology changed he'd update everything to whatever new functionality was possible. After four years there, he was given the outstanding achievement award for staff. He was so laser-focused on his coding that he hardly ever looked up long enough to get to be friends with any of his coworkers. And since, in those days, you could still smoke in your office, he spent the day drinking coffee and smoking—never eating lunch. Of course long-term, that was *such* a good approach to his heart condition and what would be a never-ending struggle with high blood pressure.

Between heat, humidity, caffeine and nicotine, it seemed like his blood would boil at the slightest irritation. And when he had to hide such irritations at work, he would generously bring them home to me. I could never decide which was worse—the days when he would bite my head off for reasons sometime completely mysterious to me, or the week that would go by without his ever saying a word to me. I certainly had no gift discerning what would set off the response one way or the other.

I was glad when our neighbors, Edouard and Edolia, would invite us over because he always tended to leave the ragin' part of the Cajun at home on such occasions. Edouard also smoked, and so he and Miles could puff away while we played bridge. We three men also liked martinis so we always drank martinis as we played. Edolia, like me, did not smoke, but neither did she drink.

She was Cajun through and through, and while I'd help in the kitchen since we always ate at their house—our apartment being too small for a bridge-and-dinner evening—she really didn't need my help. Everything she made was delicious. When her dad would visit, his Cajun accent was so thick you could barely understand him, but with my natural gift toward dialect, I got to where I could sound just like him. My imitations always amused Miles.

As much as the university liked Miles, I don't think he ever liked them much. He definitely respected some whom he considered did their job well and only pushed him to do things for the right reasons. The list was longer for those he thought of as basically useless, who as he put it, "would have me tie their shoes for them to save them the trouble of bending over."

Either he knew exactly when to finally let up, or the grace of my Hope Mennonite upbringing kicked in strong enough that any temptation I had to move out was only that—a temptation. Sometimes a *mighty* temptation! One day after church—probably three or so years into our time in Baton Rouge—we got into some tizzy over nothing on the drive home which resulted in the all too frequently used two words screamed at someone in rage.

We pulled up to a red light which I knew stayed red a long time. After a bit of silence I said, "If we are going to make it together, we have to promise that we never express that kind of contempt for each other ever again."

Miles said, "You're right."

And so it was that our vows of "for better or for worse" now had another unwritten codicil that forbade swearing at each other— period. No exceptions. My advice to others would be, worry less about a pre-nup and join us in never swearing at each other. We kept that vow to the end.

When it wasn't blazing hot or pouring down rain, we drove the Spitfire whenever the two of us went anywhere together. I drove then as often as not. We loved to get on the interstate in the late evening with the top down and you could feel cooler air descend as you got further out in the country. One spot in particular seemed to pull in just a bit of cooler night air from the surrounding countryside.

Miles had the exciting experience of driving downtown once when the brakes went completely out. Thanks to the manual transmission, he was able to keep from wrecking it or killing someone and got safely into a garage. They didn't seem too thrilled having to look at a foreign car but relented. He had no way of getting ahold of me until I was back home in the evening where he could finally get me by phone. He sat there most of the afternoon getting madder with each hour that passed.

When I finally got there to pick him up, he had not cooled down. "I'm about ready to sell that damn thing. No one ever wants to work on it, and no one ever has the damn parts!"

I thought it mostly best to stay quiet and get some crab into the boy. On the way home I pulled into our favorite little dive, and you could see him brighten up even though, by god, he wasn't in any mood to thank me for either the ride or the good idea for supper.

A couple of days later the old gal was fixed and I dropped him off to pick her up. Unfortunately, two weeks later the gears started to grind, and got worse and worse, until the only way to shift it was to hit in exactly the right spot to get it from one gear to the next. The mechanic said the master cylinder was shot and he'd have to track one down somewhere—it might take a while.

Miles said to him, both in frustration and somewhat in jest, "I don't suppose you'd like to buy it from me?"

And the mechanic, who had a couple MGs in the shop said, "I'll give $600 for it."

Miles said, "Sold."

This time when I picked him up, the mood I expected after that last breakdown wasn't there. I just waited for him to decide when to break the ice.

He said, "We don't have to go back and pick it up. I got the title out of the glove box and he gave me a check for $600."

I was very disappointed but didn't tell him so. I knew why he did it, and maybe an easier time in our lives would have brought with it the patience to get through her high maintenance needs. But we were not in those days now.

I did say, "Well, at least you got a hundred dollars more than you paid for her."

That wasn't altogether true as just before the brakes went out we'd bought four new tires and a new top. Without even a small dent, the red, shiny Spitfire looked like a finely restored vehicle.

We talked about what to do next and decided nothing was the best course of action for the moment. The apartment was close enough to the university that he could walk or bike to work very easily. We could save plenty by not having to finance a car and pay for gas and insurance.

To that idea he added, "We're buying new when we do get something else, and there has to be a dealer in every town for whatever kind it is. I'm tired breaking down and hoping the junkyards out back have what we need."

My Mennonite sense of gratitude kicked in. "At least the one time we needed it most, the junkyard out back *did* have what we needed."

Miles said, "That *was* a miracle."

Chapter Twenty-nine

We got along fine as a "one-car family." We both had good bikes and both had grown up wearing our bikes out. Since I wasn't going to have a car my freshman year at Anderson, my parents had bought me a new ten-speed which was a huge surprise. I remembered a certain Christmas when I'd talked about our Lutheran neighbors' organ they had in the house and how much fun I thought it was. That Christmas Eve, I opened one of my gifts to find a harmonica. I looked at in some bewilderment as to "why this?"

Dad said, "You said you liked organs so I got you a mouth organ."

We'll just leave it there and note he did a lot better with the new bike! I was thrilled.

It was many years later when I thought about that harmonica and Dad's singing of the cowboy songs, it dawned on me how much he probably liked the sound of the harmonica. I'm sure it must have been a disappointment to him I never made any effort to learn to play it. Sorry, Dad.

Miles bought his own bike in Anderson once we were living together off campus—so that he and I could both ride to school as time and weather allowed and not have to deal with parking and buying gas. I had a bike rack for the back of the Torino and the bikes came with us to Baton Rouge.

So far the Torino, while not aging too gracefully from too much salt on the roads in Ohio and Indiana, was sound mechanically. I, too, thought we'd buy new when the time came, but certainly wanted to get some of my Anderson debt paid off before going in any deeper.

Our main transport to and from the apartment to LSU was the bikes. The car was for transport to my job and any other running around that had to be done.

Our frugality was at least affording us some opportunities to eat out more often and go to movies. When the movie *Gandhi* came out we went to see it the first night it opened. Then, we went the next weekend to see it again. In both cases the theatre was practically empty.

I said to Miles, "What a pity. More people need to see this—especially some of our good Christian brothers and sisters."

We went a third time just after it had won a number of Academy Awards, and the theatre was packed.

Miles said, "You got your wish—a lot of people are here now."

My "no idol" Mennonite kicked in—"Too bad it took a golden idol to get them here."

On one of our movie nights we went to see a film, *Making Love*, with Kate Jackson, Michael Ontkean and Harry Hamlin. Hamlin would be more popular later, but then the only one we really knew of was Kate Jackson. We knew what the movie was about, but I wasn't sure most there had any idea.

Miles and I tended to always sit with one seat between us at movies when crowd size allowed, mostly for comfort but also to avoid inevitable disapproving glares from people gawking at two men sitting together. In this case, before going in, I suggested two chairs between us. Miles agreed this was a good idea.

The theatre was well over half full (Kate Jackson, of *Charlie's Angels* fame, being the draw we'd guessed), and we were sitting about a third of the way down—right in the center where we figured no one would crawl over us to sit between us.

At the first realization in the crowd that the couple in the movie had a fundamental flaw in their marriage—the husband being gay—fifteen to twenty people walked out. The looks as they passed in the aisle could only be described as disgust. I'm sure they went out and demanded their money back. When the two men kissed, even we were surprised by the loud, unison, "EEUUWWWHHH!" The theatre all but emptied out leaving fewer than twenty of us to stick through to the credits.

As soon as we were out of the theatre, Miles said, "Them's my peeps!" This was his catch-all phrase he would use anytime he wanted to call out bad behavior of his fellow Louisianans.

I said, "I'm not so naive as to think my fellow Buckeyes would have done differently. They just would have less drawl in their 'EEWWW.'"

118

Our most exotic movie outing was to go to our first XXX-rated film. *Debbie Does Dallas* was playing at the "adult" cinema near downtown. We decided we might as well enlighten ourselves to this part of the "culture."

We had realistic expectations going in. We were used to the stale popcorn smell and shabbiness older theatres take on over the years. We expected this to be several levels worse, and it was. We were torn as to where to sit. Near the back we thought might be really bad as we speculated some of what had gone on there over the years. Down front made any escape harder and made us more visible to any if we walked out early. The good thing about the dim-lit place was being seen and recognized was nearly impossible. The bad thing was there was no way to inspect your seat before sitting down in it. We opted for halfway down off to one side.

Miles said, "We should have brought some painter's drop cloths to sit on."

We both sat down very slowly as though somehow the ickiness of the place wouldn't transfer itself to us that way.

There was a short film before the feature. Of course, we didn't expect a great plot. A nonexistent one did surprise us some. Surely the feature, *Debbie Does Dallas,* would be better than this. We both sat there motionless so as to not have even an iota more contact with the seats than necessary, and not looking at each other—just stared at the screen.

I finally leaned over to Miles. "Are we staying for some reason in particular?"

He said, "I don't know what we're staying for."

With that he got up, and I followed right behind. Back in the car he said, "I had no idea sex could be *that* boring."

I said, "I don't know about you, but I'm going home and throwing my clothes in the washer and taking a shower. Until I do, I'm going to feel like I'm covered in ick and sleaze."

He laughed and said, "I was thinking *exactly* the same thing!"

That was the end of our XXX-rated movie adventures. We started stocking up our video collection with films a bit more our taste than the porn theatre offered—*African Queen, Gandhi, Judgment at Nuremberg, A Man for All Seasons, Keys of the Kingdom, Oliver, To Kill a Mockingbird* and *On Golden Pond.* We'd watch a couple of these every weekend until we could practically quote them word for word. We worked a number of lines from each into our own colloquial conversations.

I told Miles, "The first two dogs we get are going to be Jem and Scout. I want to go to the back door like Atticus and call out, 'Jem, Scout, come on in.'"

When I'd put dinner on the table, he'd like to quote a line from *Oliver*, "These sausages is moldy!"

Knowing I'd come back with Fagan's line, "Shut up and drink your gin!"

A favorite, but infrequent, outing was to drive down to New Orleans for a weekend of thoroughbred racing. We were real gamblers. Miles always bet two dollars on the favorite to "show." I always did a two-dollar "exacta" on longer odds. Over the course of the program, he'd almost break even, and I'd almost always lose on all ten or twelve races. The few times I did win something made us about even overall.

One time I thought I hit the jackpot. My two long-odds horses came in first and second and in the right order for my winning ticket. I was just waiting on the "official" light to come on to go collect my big winnings. Instead, the red "objection" light lit up and flashed on and off for the longest time. Finally, it went off and the board reshuffled the line-up with the "official" light coming on. The announcer said the first place horse was disqualified because the jockey had interfered with another rider. I just looked at Miles with disappointment and disgust—and took my ticket and dramatically ripped it in half letting it fall to the floor.

"That's my last exacta," I said. Adding, "I guess I'll have to join you and stick to old-lady bets," which is what our Episcopalian neighbor friend called Miles' bets when he and his wife went with us once to the races.

Chapter Thirty

Our transportation by bicycle afforded us a slower, more visible view of our immediate neighborhood, and we often waved to one retired couple just down the street who were constantly working in the beautiful cottage garden that surrounded three sides of their quaint, colorful house. One cool Saturday morning we were out riding slowly, just enjoying the brief respite from the heat and humidity. We stopped in front of their house. This was how we first met Edourd and Edolia.

Miles started in. "You have an incredible place! We love riding past to see what's in bloom."

Edouard said, "Would you like to come in and take a closer look?"

I asked, "You wouldn't mind?"

Edolia, with her think Cajun accent said, "Laissez les bon temps rouler."

I'm sure she said this to see if either of us had any Cajun roots— though not a very foolproof method. I learned that the first trip we made to New Orleans— "Let the good times roll."

Miles just said, "Well, all right then!"

With the cool day and the friendly Cajun neighbors, my Cajun left the ragin' hidden away and was happier than I'd seen him in a long time. The tour of the garden led to a tour of the house. They were such an awesome, hospitable couple. Edolia insisted we join them for gumbo and potato salad which they were going to have for lunch. It didn't take any arm twisting on our part. Edouard, had only a slight Cajun accent and was now retired. The very Cajun, Edolia, hadn't lost any of the dialect she grew up around.

We had a very nice visit over lunch and introduced a sliver of our family histories. Their children were grown now and scattered all over. None were in Louisiana. One was even in Saudi Arabia with his family working for an oil company. Some were better visiting than others. With their garden, they were never keen to leave it for very long.

After lunch we retired to the patio out back which overlooked their substantial vegetable garden, and there was a large fig tree to each side of the patio.

Miles said, "My mom used to make fig preserves every year. August grew up with raspberry preserves his mom made, and we grew up on figs."

I said, "I never had fig preserves—never even had a Fig Newton until Miles bought some back in Anderson. Unfortunately, I do love them now! I could eat a whole pack. Since Miles' mom died while we were in college, I still haven't had any fig preserves."

If they were curious about our arrangement and how we got together, there was no indication of it. Edolia disappeared back into the house for a few minutes. Edouard and I talked gardens as I described our near football-field-sized garden to him. When Edolia reappeared she had a tray with a dish of fig preserves and some French bread slices.

She said, "Here, August. You can try your first homemade fig preserves."

I said, "I'm full from gumbo and potato salad, but I'll make room."

Miles made up one slice for me and one for himself—and then a second for each of us. With that he looked at Edolia and said, "Ç'est bon!"

I said to Edolia, "That's the first time I've heard him say that for anything besides a crab boil or crab imperial."

It seemed like we were slowly becoming stand-ins for their absent family. They were old enough to be our grandparents. The morning visit had turned into an afternoon visit and was still going.

About 4:30, Edouard asked, "Any chance you boys might want a martini? I'm going to have one."

I said, "We've really imposed on your day enough already. We should be going."

Edolia said, "You don't have to on our account."

Miles repeated her earlier line, "Laissez les bon temps rouler!"

Edouard smiled, got up and was off to make the drinks. He came back with three martinis and an orange soda pop.

Edolia said, "I don't know how you all can drink that gasoline."

Over drinks and fig preserves, which all four of us continued to pick at until both the bread and figs were gone, they asked if we ever played bridge. When we said we'd heard of it but didn't know the first thing about it, Edolia got up to get some cards.

After explaining the basics, Edouard dealt a hand. "Just lay it down, and we'll count the points and what would be logical bidding."

We did that a few times with different hands. They had a little "cheat sheet" for bidding that they gave us to take home if we wanted it. That first afternoon we never played a hand—just looked at the point counts and bidding.

When we finally were excusing ourselves from imposing anymore on the little bit of their day that remained, they wondered if we wanted to come over the next Saturday around 4:00 for bridge, martinis and dinner.

I said, "We wouldn't turn it down. What can we bring?"

From the conversation, they already knew that our small under-furnished apartment did not afford us the opportunity to return their hospitality by inviting them to our place.

Edolia said, "You don't have to bring anything but yourselves."

Miles responded, "We can't make a habit of coming over here empty-handed if you keep inviting us over for bridge. But for now we'll have the good sense just to say 'thank you' and get back home."

The next Saturday turned into a weekly affair unless they or we couldn't for some reason. We were all content to rotate mostly between three main courses—ribeyes, gumbo and étouffée. As good as Bella's Gumbo recipe was, there was no way I was going to try to compete with Edolia's Cajun cooking. I did persuade them on steak night to let us bring the steaks, and in those days I made a great potato salad so I brought that with some frequency as well.

As it turned out, Edouard and I shopped at the same meat market, Thibodeaux Boucherie, so I knew the steaks we'd get were the same as he'd have bought. The owner always waited on me. When I'd approach the counter he'd say, "Koman sa va?"

And I'd answer, "Comme ci comme ça," and hope he didn't wander any further into his native Cajun French.

The first time I went to get some for bridge night, I told him I was getting steaks for dinner at Edouard's.

He said, "I know just how he likes 'em cut which is the same way you order yours—ribeyes, about an inch and a quarter."

After that when I'd go in I'd just say, "Four Edouard steaks," or "Two Kibler steaks," depending on the weekend. I was a regular Friday afternoon shopper.

And he'd say, "Okay, Slick."

I don't how I got the nickname "Slick," but I did. He certainly knew my last name from my habit of ordering and he probably knew my first name from my credit card, but he never called me by name. He did have a second nickname for whenever he handed me the finished package along with two wrapped beef bones.

"Here you go, Cool Breeze. And lagniappe pour deux chiens."

With the steaks he always gave me "that little extra for two dogs." And with my best Cajun accent I'd say, "Laissez les bon temps rouler."

Of course, we didn't have two dogs then and he never asked if we did or not. It was as much a gift for beef stock, I'm sure in his mind, and he just wanted to give a loyal customer that little extra.

At the bridge table it was always Edouard and I and Miles and Edolia as partners. We'd get right into bridge playing when we arrived, add martinis to the mix at about 5:00, stop around 6:30 for dinner, and then play several more hands after dinner—sometimes not quitting until 11:00 which was way past all our bedtimes.

We really looked forward to Saturday nights and the ragin' Cajun almost always left the ragin' companion home. After we spent so much time with them in their home, they did begin to really free up around us, and I learned soon enough that Edouard had his own ragin' Cajun. I had to admit I found it entertaining. Seeing the old married couple spar was a good reminder that irritations may not ever go away, but they don't have to overtake your lives altogether.

Edouard's older sister, Alice, was up from New Orleans once for a visit, and the three of them were sitting in the front garden when we rode up on our bikes. She looked like a breeze would blow her over. We had stayed in the garden visiting for a while when a man came through the gate uninvited. He just took over the conversation though he didn't seem to be there with any purpose. I assumed he had some connection with our friends, but nothing in the conversation seemed to indicate such was the case. Edouard finally told him we were there to help them with something in the house, and we needed to go.

The instant we got in the house, Alice said, "He's a weirdo."

I asked Edouard, "Do you know him? I've never seen him in the neighborhood before."

"Never seen him before in my life," Edouard responded.

Miles said to Edolia, "I was sure you'd invite him to stay for dinner."

Edolia in her most serious mode said, "And I was sure I wouldn't invite that couillon!"

Alice, who was an artist said, "I could paint a sign for the gate while I'm here that reads, 'Enter by invitation only' but that would assume he can read. We know he can talk."

We decided to forego bridge that evening and just visit with Alice. She was delightful and several years older than her "baby brother." Her late husband had been a geological engineer and worked around the world. They never had children and used their free time to explore any region where they found themselves.

You could hear in all her stories her affection for the indigenous peoples they met in their travels. "We were a lot more interested in the villages than we were touring another palace in some big city.

"No matter how poor, we always found kind and generous hearts. Several times we were invited to come into their home to share a meal. It was all hand gestures and smiles. We had no common words between us, but we had respect for them and that seemed to be the only language needed."

Then she shifted tone a bit. "My husband was troubled more and more as the years went by. On the one hand his work brought needed resources to areas struggling to survive in our world, but with it, he could see the ever-larger corporations exploiting at every opportunity—land and people. He had no influence changing things from the inside—try as he might. When the company he worked for was bought for the third time by a transnational behemoth, he said, 'That's it! I'm done.' He retired early and we stayed in Malaysia for several years before coming back home."

I said to Miles when we got back home, "Haven't we lived an exciting life compared to hers?"

He responded, "Yea, I can see the two of us going into some poor family's home where we don't speak a word of their language and making an evening of it!" Then he added , "She's like a walking sunbeam. Light just radiates from her."

To which I added, "You look at someone like her and it's almost impossible to imagine how life could ever leave her. If there is anything for me which is a confirmation of the idea of 'souls', it is a creature like her where you know the life *must* keep going *somehow*. Probably goofy to say it, but impossible *not* to feel it's somehow true."

Chapter Thirty-one

One of the first hymns I had learned at Park Place was a true Church of God classic.

O Church of God, the day of jubilee has dawned so bright and glorious for thee. Rejoice, give thanks, the Shepherd has begun his long divided flock again to gather into one.

The first Sunday we were in Baton Rouge we naturally went to the Church of God, and we sang it that morning. They had a pretty good choir—not Park Place but better than most. We both talked to the director after church and started going to practice right away. My class schedule interfered, but when the director learned I could pick up pretty much anything and sing it, he didn't mind me singing on Sundays even if I missed rehearsal— which was more the case than not. Miles would bring the music home, so I always had a chance to look it over and be ready.

We honored my mother's request and let it be known that Miles and I had sung a number of duets at Park Place. At our new church, we were frequently the special music at both Sunday mornings and evenings. Sometimes it was just Miles doing a solo—though usually a duet, and I never did a solo. By then, I turned them down if I was asked and would refuse even if it was just one line in a song the choir was doing.

The preacher was disappointing. He seemed to think the less you have to say the longer you should say it. He'd drone on for a good thirty-five minutes. I'd give my Cliff Notes version to Miles in the car on the way back to the apartment. Almost always, I could summarize it in one line. "Aren't we special?" The exceptions to those one-sentence summations were the real problem.

Unbeknownst to us, some resolution passed at the annual Church of God Convention which coincided with our graduation. It was sinking teeth into a doctrine where the likes of Miles and I needed to know our place. The language of the resolution was clear —no one was to be gay and be in any leadership position. If you were honest, you were out.

The exceptions to my one-sentence Cliff Notes summaries were those topics, which seemed to consume more and more of his sermons, where he was extolling the virtues of these "purifications of God's church." It wasn't that I couldn't summarize his point in one sentence. Rather, it left me speechless and neither of us could talk about it. Instead of "gathering us into one," our Church of God was peeling us off slowly but surely. As he ratcheted up the frequency and volume, we left madder and madder until we finally said, "Enough of this!"

Our several-year journey with the Church of God had come to an end. We would leave behind hymns we'd learned to love, and a history of inclusion we thought would only expand in time, and so many friends and people back in Anderson we respected enormously. It's no stretch to say it broke our hearts to leave—not that particular congregation, but the larger church which seemed to be following the national obsession with dividing "us" and "them." We had always been impressed that the church had, from its start, ordained women. In our Anderson days, we thought it would only be a matter of time before the likes of us would be fully integrated into ministry. Racially they seemed way ahead of most. However, women weren't faring much better in reality. In the early 1900s a third of the ordained were women. By the late 1900s it was down to two percent. When the denomination took the sharp turn it did as it entered the 80s, we could no longer feel at home there. And so, we started to go to the church of the "holy smoke."

Without going into any detail, one evening we said to Edouard and Edolia we were in the mood to shop for a different church. They were Episcopalians. Edolia, like Miles, grew up Catholic in New Iberia. Edouard was a cradle Episcopalian from New Orleans. They'd met right after he graduated with his engineering degree when he did some work out at Avery Island and was staying in New Iberia. Edolia was working at the hotel he called his "home away from home" over the weeks of the project. By the time they were engaged, Edouard had a job in Baton Rouge, and they'd been there ever since. They lived in an apartment for a year, and when the first child was to come along they bought the house. Edolia was quite content to stay home with the kids, get started on her passion for gardens and cook up a storm. Edouard's good job afforded them a comfortable life and enough to help their kids get a start on theirs.

Edouard said, "We told all our kids, 'The first two years of college are on us so long as you work part-time. By your junior year, you need to be on track to graduate on time and pick up at least half of your expenses.' We hoped that would wean them slowly enough that by the time they were out, they wouldn't be back here hat-in-hand expecting to live off of us. If they didn't want to go to college, we'd figure out some way of helping them along in a similar fashion with whatever it was they wanted to work at to give them a jump-start in life. All five ended up going to college."

Back at the apartment I said to Miles, "I was really glad to hear Edouard use the "we" pronoun as he talked about the support of their kids. I've heard plenty of men who call themselves the 'breadwinner' who would never include their wife in the financial equation if she was home like Edolia has been all these years."

"I noticed that too," he said. "Must be why we like those two. Not like that brother of mine who is always, 'I—I—I' and always refers to his latest wife as 'my woman.'"

I added, "And I liked that they didn't insist college was the only option."

As they shared with us their church lives these days, Edolia went when the mood struck her which wasn't very often. As she told it, she'd been better about attending when the kids were home. Once they were gone she said, "I'd rather sit quietly in the garden."

Edouard was faithful every Sunday at the early, 8 o'clock mass. He was also the very-faithful eucharistic minister assisting the priest. As there were no young children at the early service, he said, "And I'm probably the oldest living acolyte since I light the candles too."

I told them, "Back in Anderson, Miles and I would attend the Saturday evening Catholic mass every now then and always passed a very attractive Episcopal church. I was curious then, but not knowing anyone there or anything about the church, we never tried it. I did ask someone once about the Episcopal church—her dad was a minister and so I thought she might know something about it as he was involved in the local ministerial association."

"'They're a cult,' was all she said."

Before I got a chance to go on with my account Edouard and Edolia, on hearing this, laughed so hard I thought both were going to wet themselves.

I then added what I was planning to before their outburst of laughter, "I chalked her up as an unreliable source of information as I at least knew it had a long history in this country. Truthfully, my only hesitation was the notion I had that it might be a rather closed, upper-crust community. I thought we might feel out of place."

They both laughed at that too. He knew of our love of music and said, "If you're brave enough to join us cultists and elitists some Sunday, you should try the 10:30 service. We don't have music at 8:00, but 10:30 has a lot of music."

We knew Edouard had once been in a barber shop chorus and so I was curious about why he went to an all-spoken service.

"I just like to get-in and get-out early so I have the rest of the day here."

When we went the next Sunday to the 10:30, the high church service blew us both away. Miles thought he'd died and gone to heaven, as it reminded him of the mass in Franklin when he was a boy before the informality of the "guitar mass" took over—a development he didn't care for. For me, it was about as un-Mennonite as I could imagine—but so festive and dramatic, I had an inherent attraction to it.

Given all the incense I asked Miles, "Are we going to finally leave the Church of God and attend the church of the holy smoke?"

Unfortunately, he saw this as an opportunity to suggest my hypocrisy, saying, "Oh, so smoke in the church is okay but smoke in the apartment isn't."

I said, "I was about to choke, but unlike your cigarettes, their incense smells pretty good—and I don't have to smell it in the shower every morning."

I knew that was the wrong answer if I wanted to keep him from flipping on his "anger switch," but it was an honest one and nothing came quick enough to me to say anything else. Fortunately, he was only a little bit annoyed since he knew he was the one who took the conversation in that direction—setting himself up for what irritated him most—me nagging him about his smoking.

The next Sunday we were back and continued going as long as we lived in Baton Rouge.

When we first announced to a friend at the Church of God that we were now attending our neighbors' Episcopal church, she said, "Why would you join the Whiske'palians?"

"Obviously you don't know as much about Episcopalians as you think," I said. "They drink gin martinis and so do we, so we fit right in." Then I added, "If you really have to ask why we're leaving with the sermons you hear on Sunday, then I guess you are totally clueless as to how he makes Miles and me feel."

She said, "Have you talked to him about your concerns?"

Knowing her inherent dislike of confrontation, I answered her question with a question, "Would you?" Adding, "This much I know about human nature. When one has glued an ideology to their job security, the chances for that person to understand another are nonexistent. I don't know if he even really believes what he preaches, but I have no doubt he believes he has 'true believers to the cause' sitting in the pews. As long as he feeds them what they crave his job is secure. This, it seems to me, is what Jesus meant when he said of the scribes and pharisees, 'When you have made a convert, you make them twice as fit for hell as you are yourself.'

"He has fed them empty calories for so long, they no longer know what real food tastes like."

"That's pretty harsh," she said, taking it a bit personally.

"It's only harsh if it's not true," I said. "It is for you to discern if it is true or not."

Perhaps she didn't like the self-evaluation my words would require of her. Perhaps she was more "true believer" than we'd imagined. Or perhaps once we didn't attend anymore we just naturally drifted apart. Whatever the reason or combination of reasons, we never heard from her again.

Our busy schedules and our own preordained plans to leave Baton Rouge as soon as I graduated gave us permission, in our own minds, to attend the church of the holy smoke without having to join or get too involved. We could do that down the road—when we were more settled into life with an eye more towards some fidelity to place. We never joined the choir or attended many church functions. We were faithful Sunday morning attendees and not much more.   Attending also gave us a nice topic of shared interest to add to our Saturday evening bridge gatherings.

Chapter Thirty-two

Since first meeting Alice, we got to see her on two other trips she made from New Orleans, where she lived in the old family home where she and Edouard had been raised—right in the Garden District.

Edouard had said once, "Don't picture one of those mansions on St. Charles—think shotgun house south a few blocks."

Once the four of us made a trip to New Orleans to attend the horse races, and so we got to see both Alice and the family home. The house seemed to take on her personality—it was light and charming.

Edouard knew how drawn we were to Alice and was sure to have us over anytime she was there visiting. While we saw them all the time, we rarely if ever called each other on the phone—so when the phone rang midweek pretty late in the evening, I thought immediately something must be going on.

"August, it's Edouard. Alice was killed and we just got the word. I haven't even called any of our kids yet. The New Orleans police just called me."

"What on earth?" I exclaimed.

"You know how she liked to walk everywhere she could. A witness said some lunatic wasn't content just to steal her purse; he shoved her hard as he prepared to run off and her head split open on a light post."

I didn't know what you say to that. Miles, being the better comforter than I, probably would have thought of something; or he would have been in tears with the first pronouncement of her being killed. As it was, I flashed back to our conversation about the light in Alice—now killed hitting her head on a light post. What came out was this.

"Hate, doing its worst to the best yet again."

He ended the call saying, "She was the best."

We didn't say goodbye. I didn't say, let us know what we can do, as there was nothing we could do but be their friends. He just hung up and began repeating the story five more times for their children—and how ever many other relatives he would need to call.

Miles and I knew, without any hesitation, that we would go to New Orleans for the funeral home visitation and funeral. It would be my first Episcopal funeral. The church was packed and the service beautiful. This young Swiss Mennonite was in tears when I heard the opening words of the liturgy.

Miles said on the drive home that evening, "You could see her light still shining in every face who ever knew her. Hate had no power over her even in death."

All I could say to that was, "You do have beautiful thoughts every now and then." We drove the rest of the way home in silence.

We knew Edouard and Edolia planned to stay in New Orleans for a couple weeks to attend to Alice's estate matters, and we offered to water the garden if needed while they were gone. We weren't sure how we might proceed with our regular Saturday evening bridge nights once they returned. We knew they'd gotten back home and took one of our Saturday morning bike rides hoping they would be out in the garden, which they were.

Edolia spoke first as we sat stationary on our bikes outside the gate—not presuming we should come into the garden. "I can tell you did more than water. There wasn't a weed anywhere to be found."

Miles said, "I have a whole new appreciation for the work you put into keeping it so beautiful. While we were weeding, August said, 'Takes me back to my mom's huge garden where that rich soil attracted every kind of weed on earth.'"

Edouard said, "It sure was nice of you boys to come down to New Orleans. It meant a lot to us."

I said, "You mean a lot to us."

We'd met all their family except the family living in Saudi Arabia who couldn't make it back in time. I added, "A sad occasion, but it was nice to meet your kids and their families. You have quite a brood."

Edolia said, "Come on over this evening. I'll make a crawfish étouffée. We might as well see if we still know how to play bridge."

Edouard added, "The first martini we'll toast Alice. She'd approve of that!"

I said, "Okay. We'll see you this evening."

We did toast Alice, and while we carried on in our routine, she was with us in spirit. Edouard recalled many small, humorous tales of their childhood. One he remembered, with particular affection, was his having to try on her clothes.

He explained, "She was, of course, several years older than me, and we had a cousin my age who lived in Metairie. When we were about nine, the cousin and I were about the same size. My mom would say, 'Here, try on this dress of your sister's. If it fits you it will fit your cousin.' I bet I tried on 10 dresses over the next year or so as Alice's hand-me-downs went to her. I was glad to finally have a growth spurt that put me ahead of my cousin and Alice. Alice said, 'Edouard, you'll have to go shopping for your own dresses from here on.' Then she added, 'If you want, I might buy you a nice frock for your graduation when the time comes.' I told her, I didn't think that would be necessary. She always laughed about that."

Then he said, "I guess from now on, I'm going to think of her every time I see some high school girl in a fancy frock or a drag queen on TV at Mardi Gras. That time of our life came back to me as I looked at her in that coffin, and I had to smile at the thought of it."

For me, as time passed, I found that I'd stare at some odd light post now and then, and it would take me back to the grief and joy of the wonderful light and life of Alice.

Chapter Thirty-three

With graduation finally approaching—it took me five long years to get there—we stepped up the pace of job searches. We sure hoped we could end up in cooler climes, and focused on the opportunities in the Appalachians, having fallen in love with Asheville on our one trip there. With my graduation came the last payment of college loans. We would be leaving Baton Rouge free and clear of all debt. Oh, that was a glorious feeling!

Just at the thought of cooler climes and no debt, I felt the tension Miles and I had lived with for the past five years begin to finally disperse. I'd barely graduated when Miles got a phone interview, followed by an on-site, followed by a job offer at the university in Boone, North Carolina. There was zero hesitation. He said "yes" and gave his notice to LSU the same day; and I gave mine to the contractor.

When I told Louie, CJ and Darnell I was leaving, Louie said, "I hate to think we're going to have to try to break in someone new at our age. Lucky for us, you didn't take no breakin' in."

I said, "You have no idea the breakin' in you did. I started this job with a lot of fear of what it was going to be like for a young northern whippersnapper trying to work with an older Louisiana construction crew that was two-thirds white and one-third black. I had all manner of wild things running around in my mind of the troubles I might have. You took me in like I somehow belonged."

CJ said, "That's 'cause ya did belong."

Louie chuckled showing that gold and diamond tooth. "When I saw you on that first day I said to these two, 'Jesus said, 'Suffer the little children to come unto me.' Then I said, 'He looks a little scared comin' into this job—we're gonna make sure he ain't scared of us.' We all three agreed. Soon enough we saw a good heart behind that little bit of fear anybody would have."

I said, "I can almost count on one hand the people I'm going to miss—you three, Gloria and our two Cajun neighbors. Five years, six friends. Not sure what that says about us."

Darnell, who almost never added anything but went along with what someone else had said, piped in, "It says you'd rather really know people than line 'em up as some kinda collection to show off."

Louie said, "Darnell, you been hidin' that wisdom all these years?"

We all had a good laugh and carried on with the day's work. On my last day, we shook hands and knew we'd probably never see each other again. And we never did—except I see them in my mind as clear as day, and especially think of them every time I see a concrete pour or a retainer wall going in.

We made one last trip to Franklin to see Miles' dad before we headed north and east. I asked Miles if he wanted me to arrange a Bergeron family reunion with his brothers as well while we were there.

"I can live without it," was all he said. Of course, I knew he'd shoot down that idea as he was never eager to see them. They were masters at pushing his buttons, and they seemed hell-bent on pushing any button having to do with his making his life with another man.

I could never figure out where the boys got their rather bossy nature. I never met Bella, but by all Miles' descriptions she was slight in body—but a strong, forthright person, though in no way domineering. His dad was decidedly on the quiet and reserved side, especially for a full-blown Cajun. He'd worked as parts manager at a Chrysler-Dodge dealership for as long as Miles had been alive, except for his brief leave to do something as a military contractor during Vietnam. He had started as a shop assistant to the mechanics at the same dealership when he graduated high school.

One of the brothers did show up while we were there, and I couldn't help but notice that Mr. Bergeron didn't invite the elder son to dinner when we'd already decided we were going out that evening. The brother talked while we listened, and I had the first up-close-and-personal view of how different Miles was from his brother—and how Miles definitely leaned more towards his quieter dad.

When the brother finally got up to leave, we all stood and walked toward the door. When he was down the walk, Miles' dad turned and muttered, "That boy never shuts up."

Back in Baton Rouge, we said our goodbyes to the only people in our lives there that had really mattered to us. Miles had never attached to anyone personally at the university. They offered to hold a going away reception for him, and he told them he didn't want one. We bid farewell to Edouard and Edolia, who we would miss a great deal, and I had already said my farewells to Louie, CJ and Darnell. CJ assured me he'd pass along our best to Gloria.

On the drive to our new home I said to Miles, "In five years we never found a friend our age or had a single gay friend. If we make a habit of befriending people thirty or more years older, at some point we're going to run out of friends altogether."

We had made a modest effort with a few closer to our age, but it seemed like they were totally into themselves or liked movies and music we couldn't stand. Oh, it's not that we only liked church music, symphonies and pipe organs. We also liked Patsy Cline and Abba and Bob Marley and Randy Travis. We liked Zydeco and Blue Grass. We were pretty eclectic to our minds. But any one outing with the younger set was pretty much over after the first time. We worked under the assumption that if they called, we'd try again, but we weren't going to go pursuing them. None ever called.

After about the fifth time this happened, Miles said, "Nobody likes us."

I thought that statement needed some illumination and said, "We don't go out of our way to take up their interests. Somehow we fit right in with the older crowd, and such may be our lot in life."

Life in the Mountains

Chapter Thirty-four

Out of debt and Miles already on the job, we decided as soon as I got a job we were going car shopping. The rust spots on the Torino were getting such that the steel rattled on the doors every time you slammed them shut—and required more forceful slamming as time passed. The old rust bucket had made one road trip up for the interview, and we hoped it would make it one more time for our move—now having to pull a small U-Haul behind it. It did pretty well until the mountains, when we'd have to stop and let the engine cool back down before heading back up and down the steep grades. Thankfully it made it—it had always been a remarkably dependable vehicle if not a pretty one. What the Spitfire had in spirit, this one had in practicality.

When the job offer finally came through for me as an assistant director at the physical plant at the university, we talked about whether we could go on as a one-car family or if getting two cars— or a car and a pickup—was more practical. We decided we could always get a second if it proved too inconvenient with one.

I said, "Your first English car was so cute and reliable, I think we should get a Jaguar."

Miles had two things to say about that. "I don't think so, and no good Mennonite boy would spend that much money on a car unless he wanted his grandmother boxing his ears."

I hated when he nailed things like that. "But those black Jags are so pretty," I said.

His comeback to that was, "Buy a poster of one then, and you can hang it up and look at it as much as you want."

It didn't look like I was going to win the Jaguar exchange, which I'd assumed I wouldn't before I started. "What do you want to go look at?" I asked him.

His solution was, "We'll go to the biggest dealer in town and buy whatever is the most reliable make and model they have."

Discerning which dealership was actually the largest wasn't as easy as he thought it would be. I also wasn't sure how we were going to determine the most reliable make and model. We drove around to see what the options were on dealerships. When we'd narrowed it to a couple of different ones, we then decided we'd get out and walk around and see how pushy the sales people were. Would they let us look around? Would they give real answers or, as Miles put it, "salesman's bullshit"—a line he'd heard his dad use numerous times about some of the salespeople who came and went at the dealership where he worked.

We weren't at the first dealership long. We passed some salesperson as we drove into the lot, and I looked at him—not with any interest one way or the other but to be sure I didn't run him over. We drove up a couple hundred yards, parked and started looking around. Another salesman came up and seemed pleasant enough, just asking what we might have in mind.

Before we could answer, here comes the first guy who says to the other man, "These are *my* customers."

The other man walked away, and when he did we headed back to our car. The first guy came pursuing us. "Where are you going?"

Neither of us said a word. The best protest at such inconsiderate behavior seemed to be to move on. We got back in the car and drove away.

I wouldn't be surprised if the man heard Miles from the car when he said, "What a shit-ass!"

I said, "If we do have to come back here, we'll be sure to track down the other guy and work with him—letting the manager know of our disgust."

We didn't have to go back. The next dealer had a car we both liked for a price we liked.

On our trade he said, "I'm sorry, but we can only give you $500 on it."

Realizing it had reached its "near end of life" I said, "That's $500 more than I'd give you for it."

He said if we wanted to go have lunch and get our insurance squared away, they would have both the car and the financing ready when we got back. We'd already made contact with the insurance company, so all we had to do was give them the VIN and details—and they had a binder faxed to the dealership by the time we were back from lunch. We left the Torino with them, and as I drove by the first dealership, I saw the shit-ass salesman out there headed towards his next victim. I put down my window, blew the horn and waved. I doubted he realized who it was, but I sure hoped he did.

Within the first month, we'd found our comfortable place in our new pew in the Episcopal church. We couldn't help but notice we brought down the average age of the group. It appeared we were likely to find ourselves again with older friends, and indeed such was the case. There was no question of welcome. When we were there for our third visit and our first time to go back to the coffee hour, a small herd descended upon us. One couple invited us to go with them to lunch at the country club the next Sunday. The next, hearing their invitation, suggested we join them for dinner one evening that week if it was convenient. And a third man, there by himself, invited us to come over right then. To such an abundance of riches, we looked at the first couple and said "Sure, next Sunday sounds great;" to the second couple, "How does Thursday sound?" And to the gentleman, "We're ready when you are."

I knew it was our voices and relative young age which drew these stalwarts of the church to us. Our enthusiastic singing always did.

We followed behind the single man's Lincoln Town Car to where he pulled into a small but very neatly kept house only a few blocks from the church. As he got out of the car, he lit a cigarette. I didn't say anything to Miles but I thought, "Damn! I can't get away from these things."

We knew his name to be Winston Majors from introductions at the church. I now thought, "How appropriate. A smoker named Winston—but then this is North Carolina." Inside we met the other half of the equation.

A rather large man in a loose-fitting shirt, shorts and sandals came from the back of the house when he heard us come in the front. Winston made the introductions. "Travis, this is August Kibler and Miles Bergeron—the boys I told you have been to church a couple times. Boys, this is Travis Gensheimer."

Travis didn't even say it was nice to meet us. He went right on to what he wanted to know. "How long have you two been together?"

Miles, assuming we each had the others' number, said, "He fell in love with me our sophomore year in college and that's been eight years now. He's still holding out hope I'll fall in love with him one of these years."

I said, "Patience is one of my greatest gifts."

Travis said, "Winston is still hoping and it's been over thirty-one for us."

"That's wonderful," Miles replied.

Travis said, "Bergeron—are you a coonass?"

Winston was clearly embarrassed by Travis' rather crude question to Miles. He asked, "Can I get you something to drink?"

I said, "You are a good Episcopalian! What are you having?"

He answered, "Beefeater martini on the rocks with olives—dry."

Miles said, "Those are the magic words for us both," and addressing the coonass question said to Travis, "Yes, pure Cajun—born and raised in Franklin, Louisiana."

Travis said, "I assume anyone who shows up this time of day expects to be fed. I'll go throw something together for lunch. I'm sure there is some leftover squirrel stew somewhere in the fridge if the mold hasn't gotten to it."

We were quickly learning that Travis was a real character and a lovable curmudgeon.

Winston was soon back with the martinis, leaving one in the kitchen for Travis. He no sooner set down the drinks when he offered us a cigarette as he lit another for himself. Of course, Miles couldn't turn that down.

On the one trip my mom and dad made to Baton Rouge, Miles told Mom he was trying to cut down. Anytime he went for one she'd say, "Now, that's one you could do without."

Her words had more force than mine. When I suggested the same on this occasion I got the ragin' Cajun stare, and he lit up.

The next thing we heard was the voice from the kitchen, "Winston, set the table."

While they were in the kitchen, we looked around the room which had a number of fine antiques and several fine needlepoint—framed pieces on the walls.

Then we heard Travis again. "It's ready," was all he said.

When I saw what was on the table I said, "I guess the stew'd gone moldy. This looks tasty," and it was.

We quickly learned of our mutual interest in bridge and after clearing the table, Winston got the cards out. We first drew for partners and then for dealing. I drew Travis and Miles drew Winston. Winston drew to deal.

It had been a while since they had played. They had friends they used to play with most weekends, but the couple—who had been together even longer than they—got into arguments over what card should have been played, or what the bidding should have been and wasn't. Winston and Travis suggested several times that they partner with them instead of each other but for some reason such a suggestion was always ignored.

Travis' take on that was, "They both have to win and there is no chance of that if they aren't paired together."

Winston added, "On our last night over there playing bridge, Travis said on the way home, 'If I hear one more postmortem on a hand we've just played, I'm gonna scream!' We started making excuses why we couldn't play and eventually they quit asking. Now we just see them once in a while and that's usually in larger social gatherings."

The first couple of times the four of us played we always drew for partners. But Miles and I clued in pretty quickly during the course of playing several rubbers that to keep peace we were going to avoid the two of them being partners. We had a pretty natural style with Miles and Winston as partners, and Travis and me. From then on we'd sit in the same seats, draw to deal and play cards.

Travis would throw in the driest comments that would make us all laugh—such was his humor. Once when Winston was talking about some salad dressing he'd read about, he mentioned emulsifying it to which Travis dryly interjected, "I don't even know my emulsification tables." If we went out to eat, he'd say to Winston or whoever was driving—as he always chose to ride rather than drive—"Get me home so I can fart."

One Thanksgiving when we were over at their house for dinner, Travis was in the grumpier side of his moods. He had reasons to be that way. He lived with varying degrees of pain from being wounded badly in an ambush in Korea during the war. He was the only one of his squad to live—and barely so. He had his good days and bad. Sometimes it seemed to me, Winston hadn't learned as well as I had when to leave well enough alone. I'd gotten pretty good at knowing when to leave my ragin' Cajun be.

As we sat down to the meal that Travis had worked on all morning, standing on his feet preparing, I could see this wasn't one of his better days. Winston tried to be chipper and said, "Isn't this a wonderful day?"

Travis blurted out as dryly and seriously as he could, "I ain't never had a good day in my life."

That was a line that would never die. Miles and I would use it ourselves when we really were having a wonderful day.

Another line came from a time they were standing in the department store line and one woman asked her friend if she thought the blouse she was getting ready to buy would go with a skirt she already had. Her friend answered, "Oh, honey, I can't feature how nothin' looks with anything till I sees it together."

Some days Winston would call to see if we'd want to come over for a Saturday lunch or weekday dinner. When Miles would answer the phone he would make a point of asking, "What are we having?"

Winston would holler, "Travis, Miles wants to know what we're having."

He'd answer always the same, "Tell that coonass he's not supposed to ask, he's just supposed to be grateful he's being fed. And tell him I already have to cook three times as much because that Cajun is coming."

He really was amazed how much Miles could put away.

One night over dinner we got to talking about early days when we were all so broke we could barely feed ourselves.

I said, "There were more times than I can count where I just had coleslaw and water and Miles lived on saltines and Vienna sausage."

Travis said, "We ate so much beans and rice I got sick of seeing white rice—and added blue food coloring to make it seem like we were having something different."

Miles added, "We had plenty of rice and beans too and if we had some sausage to add to it, it was a real feast day."

We all cracked up at the common plight of our early years—looking back on such times with joy that, at the time, one couldn't imagine would bring back happy memories. It was a way, too, of realizing it could happen again through some unforeseen misfortune. None of us ever assumed the hard times of earlier years couldn't revisit us in the future.

I told the others, "Knowing that is a healthy portion of humble pie."

Another memory that worked its way into our vernacular was of a road trip where they stopped to fill up back in the days of full-service stations. The attendant started filling the tank and asked Winston, "Ya'll been eatin' chicken?"

"Pardon?" Winston asked.

The attendant repeated, "Ya'll been eatin' chicken?"

At least that's what Winston thought he said. He answered, "No," with some puzzlement as to why he'd asked.

Travis was clearly amused but was waiting until they pulled away to say anything. Winston said, "Why did he want to know if we were eating chicken?"

Travis, who grew up around thick dialects, laughed and said, "He asked, 'Da your oil be needin' checkin'' not if you'd been eatin' chicken!"

"Ya'll been eatin' chicken?" became our frequent greeting with the four of us.

Travis was a lot like Miles in temperament and smoking. Both were migrating to social smoking more than habit, which was at least some encouragement. Winston, on the other hand, was practically a chain-smoker. He would sit there hacking up a lung for two minutes, take another drag of his cigarette and hoarsely say, "Damn that's good."

They had converted part of their long garage into a pool house and put in a swimming pool not long after buying the house some twenty years earlier. Once when their real estate taxes went up,

Winston decided to file a protest. The city sent out an appraiser to take a look.

The appraiser got to the back and said, "Oh! We didn't know you had all this back here."

Instead of winning his protest their taxes went up even higher—which isn't saying much in Watauga County. As Travis put it, "He couldn't leave well enough alone—as usual."

They were certainly our closest friends and the only gay friends we ever had. With few exceptions, we spent every weekend with them doing one thing or another, and often went out to eat together during the week. We could see age catching up to both and Winston's heavy smoking catching up with him. First, he'd been diagnosed with emphysema and a year later with lung cancer.

He still didn't give up the habit saying, "I might as well go out happy."

It wasn't a very happy end. His cancer spread quickly, but took about six months of a pretty miserable time of it before hospice came in and provided the palliative care he badly needed.

Now, we attended our second Episcopal funeral. He was interred in the church's columbarium with a niche reserved next to his for Travis.

By then, Travis' brother was a widower and his nephew, recently divorced, had taken in his dad. He wanted Travis to come live with them as well which was a noble task. We had profound respect for the nephew taking on the care of two old men. He was a nurse, and they could hardly have fared better. Travis had the good sense to see such was the case, and we bade him farewell. He would sell the house and move some 800 miles from Boone. We would never see him again, though, as trustee of the columbarium, I would inter his ashes five years later.

Chapter Thirty-five

The couple we met and went to dinner with during the week of that first coffee hour were friendly, but we never got into any serious routine with them. They had family hither and yon and spent most of their time visiting grandchildren or babysitting them.

Our country-club friends, Ellery and Nan Robinson, were as close as we ever came to personally knowing millionaires. They weren't "filthy rich" but they, more than any others, ensured the church had plenty of money to keep the place up and running, and they were generous with scholarship funds at the university as well. As Ellery put it, "It is no credit to my accomplishments. I inherited every cent of it."

He had a very eccentric grandfather who never liked his two sons-in-law, so he wrote his will to bypass both them and his own daughters, leaving all his estate—which was land, stocks and bonds—to "his daughters' descendants." Ellery's aunt never married and never had a child. Ellery had one sister, so they each inherited half of the grandfather's several-million-dollar estate. When the sister died, she had no children and he ended up with what she'd left as well, though he didn't keep that. As her executor, he passed half her estate onto the university and earmarked the other half for a charity project he had in mind.

Since they were members of the country club and we were not, they treated us to Sunday brunch about once every couple months. As far as we knew, they went every Sunday. We would return the favor by taking them to dinner during the week. Also about once a month, we traded off Friday night bridge and dinner. We would be close to them, but never as close as we were to Winston and Travis.

When we first arrived in Boone, the church had a priest who had just been installed a month earlier. Miles and I had our first weird encounter with him when he had an open house at his home following a Sunday service as a celebration for his new post. He pulled Miles and me into his office where he pulled out a picture of himself in a devil's costume—complete with big, red horns on his head and holding an elaborate pitchfork. He grinned and chuckled at himself as he showed it to us. We returned rather reluctant grins and didn't know what to say. Neither of us thought he knew us well enough to assume we'd be amused. We were creeped out more than anything.

Ellery was senior warden at the time, and soon got to deal with a mess far worse than the poor fit we'd had with the minister back at Hope Mennonite all those years ago. When we would get together with Ellery and Nan, he would confide in us some of the concerns—which most of the congregation was totally unaware of at that point.

We shared with them the devil-picture incident to which Nan said, "Where there is a devil, there's fire. You can bet we're going to get burned before this is over."

Things manifested themselves in a series of escalating problems. The first was, they found out after the fact that at his last church he had gotten the congregation deeply into debt, building a new building they couldn't afford—unless the church grew, which he fooled them into believing was going to happen if they only had faith to build the new church. He soon tried the same in Boone but couldn't get any of the vestry on board with his illusions of grandeur.

Then they started to hear stories where he would visit some of the older widows or they would be in his office, and he would solicit money for his discretionary fund to help "single mothers and battered women." They were giving him cash, checks and even jewelry, and he was putting the proceeds into his discretionary account sure enough—but it was never going out to its promised recipients. The church secretary clued Ellery in about the money coming in, and his stash of jewelry in his desk drawer, and no apparent needy women ever showing up as he'd led everyone to believe. Something was off. At this point, Ellery pulled the bishop into the situation as they tried to figure out what exactly he was doing with the money. The priest asserted his right to keep the account confidential for "the sake of the women involved." He would offer a bank statement to the treasurer each month, redacted in black as to whom the outgoing checks were made to.

Ellery and Nan never could figure out if the wife, who seemed sweet enough, was clueless to this or in cahoots with him. As time progressed, they began to think the latter was the case, but never did know for sure. One thing was for sure—he was a pathological liar. I told them of the old cuss who my dad had said would lie even when the truth sounded better.

Things were moving far more slowly than Ellery liked, but too many on the vestry wanted to "keep him on and work things out." The bishop respected this approach, though to us it looked more like procrastination and having no clue what to do with him if forced out. Almost two years after his installation, it finally came to an abrupt end when his name appeared in the Boone police blotter—arrested for indecent exposure. The bishop forced his immediate resignation and sent him off for some clearly needed psychiatric help. From what we'd gathered, that didn't last long. He and his wife vanished from sight, and we never did know whatever became of them. We did have one parishioner who took it upon herself to write to every bishop in the country to warn them about him. Whether that was needed or did any good was pretty questionable, but she felt she'd done what she needed to for her own conscience—since she had been one who was resistant to booting him out early on.

With Ellery still senior warden and Nan on the search committee, both were determined to ensure a far more rigorous search. The committee and vestry took their time and, as Nan put it, "We'll risk boring sermons over hiring another sociopath."

And that is sorta what we got. The new rector and his wife were gentle, sweet people, but dynamic they were not. They wouldn't have to worry about him spending them into debt. He seemed perfectly content with everything the way it was and didn't rock the boat in any sense of the term. He had harmless sermons— never offending and rarely inspiring. As important as music was in the parish, he couldn't carry a tune and didn't try to. He wasn't low church or high church. From time to time for solemn or festive Sundays, he would bring out the incense and draft Miles to serve as cantor.

Immediately following his installation, Ellery asked if I would take over as treasurer. The only obstacle was the rector knew I wasn't confirmed and so was "not a member in good standing." To proceed, I would have to be confirmed.

I didn't want to disappoint Ellery, but I wasn't thrilled at the idea of confirmation either. I had grown fond of the notion in the

Church of God of no membership—even though they did, in fact, require you to resister if you wanted to vote in congregational affairs. "Membership" was one obstacle to me; but the greater was the fact that as a Catholic, Miles would be "received" which consisted of the bishop shaking his hand and welcoming him to the Episcopal Church. I, as a Mennonite, would have to undergo "instruction" and be confirmed. I thought then and would always hold that this was just absurd. The only thing I got out of my instruction was the validation of what I already knew. Episcopalians have too many damn rules, plenty of which the clergy and bishops use or misuse at their convenience.

I at least halfway liked the bishop at the time, who had finally gotten rid of the troubled priest. So for Ellery and Nan, and so I could "be in good standing," I was confirmed and made treasurer—which I continued to be until we parted company years later. I was no sooner confirmed than the bishop announced his retirement and they brought in another. This one might just well have been a Fortune 500 CEO. He ran things efficiently, it must be said, if not charitably or on the high side of the ethical curve. He'd know my disapproval of how they managed their affairs when they made the mistake of putting me on one of the diocesan committees. I was short-lived in that appointment—I resigned for matters of conscience.

Chapter Thirty-six

We told Ellery and Nan that we'd enjoyed the horse races in New Orleans and they said they always watched the triple crown races every year. We started a regular routine of going to their house on Derby, Preakness and Belmont race day for day-long bridge and racing. Ellery was our "bookie." We would forego our usual martinis or G&Ts for mint juleps in silver goblets which, for whatever reason, I was charged with making for the four of us. Miles and I always took a big bouquet of flowers along with us— red roses for Derby day, black-eyed Susans for the Preakness, and white carnations for the Belmont.

One time when Nan's recently divorced sister was visiting, she asked if I would make her a virgin mint julep. She'd never had one she said, and no longer drank alcohol. My mischievous self said enthusiastically, "Sure, be glad to." I knew instantly what I was going to do.

I arrived back a few minutes later with the five silver goblets. She looked at hers as I was setting the tray down on the lid of the grand piano, leaned to her sister and whispered, "I think August forgot to fill mine."

Nan took one look and started to laugh. She had wondered what I was going to do to make a virgin mint julep, but figured I knew of some substitution. I had put in all the crushed ice and topped it with a sprig of mint. She said, "Sister, a mint julep is mint and pure bourbon. You got everything there but the bourbon."

My unwitting victim looked at me smiling and said, "You're a little too pleased with yourself—making a fool of an old lady." Then she laughed even harder than the rest of us at the trick I'd played on her. "I'll just sit here and sip my ice as it melts!"

Nan said when her sister would call after that visit, she would relay the latest person she'd told about her virgin mint julep. Nan said, "She always did like to tell on herself and laugh about it. You've given her new material for her act."

A year into my confirmation and treasurership, Ellery's rather elusive account of the other half of his sister's estate came to light. Not trusting the priest at the time, he'd somehow—with his attorney's help—parked it aside as charitable to avoid any tax on it, and now moved it officially in the church accounts where it was to be used to rebuild and expand the old pipe organ. All the priest and the church were to know was that this was possible from an anonymous bequest. Just enough time had passed, and most didn't seem to put two and two together. His sister was not a member of the church so they didn't know her or anything about her estate.

I rounded up a loaner Rodgers organ while the old organ was completely disassembled and rebuilt adding several new ranks. A year and a half later it was dedicated by the bishop.

I told the priest, "The bequest stipulated that at the dedication the hymns sung were to include *Lift High the Cross* and *Christ Is Made the Sure Foundation*."

I fibbed slightly as there was nothing about hymns in Ellery's gift. I did know their favorite hymns, though, and so it was with delight that they heard both at the dedication. I was sitting next to Ellery on the aisle and Miles was down the pew next to Nan. When Ellery heard that opening hymn, he had tears running down his cheeks as the crucifer passed us in the aisle.

They'd never had children, and Ellery said more than once he thought it was a good thing his family line was dying out—as he thought losing one's mind ran in the family. He did get somewhat muddled in his old age but not significantly more than most. In their sixty-five years of marriage, neither lived with any regret about not having children. They enjoyed life and saw to it the children they never had might get a helping hand—they left their entire estate to the scholarship fund he had set up in his sister's name. Nan had a niece and a nephew who felt quite violated as they had long assumed they would be the rightful heirs. In this regard, the only thing I would ever do unwillingly for them was serve as executor of their estate. I didn't mind when they first asked, but after Ellery died and Nan just three months later, the vultures descended. I would have considerable hell getting them to fly off once and for all. I did try to give them some personal items like their wedding photos. As I would discover when I carried the trash cans to the curb, they both had chucked them in the trash.

I said to Miles, "Too bad Nan's only sister had children—and two nasty ones at that."

Miles said, "I don't have to wonder now why she was divorced. If those kids were anything like their father, she had a hell of life while she was married with the three of them in the house."

A few years into the rector's tenure, the church brought in Christina from Charlotte as their first curate. She was wonderful. I was a little concerned early on that the rector would envy her talents, as she was a colorful preacher and had a perfect voice for chanting. He let her add as much of that as she wanted in the service, so she started chanting the Gospel lesson each Sunday—and when she would celebrate mass, much of the liturgy as well. Her sermons drew you in to real stewardship—not in the monetary sense, but in terms of respect for human dignity and the created world. She had a way of making you feel, like on your drive home, if you saw trash along the road, you should stop and pick it up. If you were looking at "sale" items at a store, you didn't need to keep walking.

A new family wandered in one Sunday and were so taken by Christina, they kept coming back. It must be said, we were all taken with them as well. They were delightful and brought new life to the place! With Christina and the family, we seemed to be awakening from a somewhat dull routine. As the new family told their friends about Christina, before we knew it we had—for the first time in ages in that church—as many under forty as over. Since she lived in our duplex the five years she was there, and because I seemed soldered as treasurer, she and I kept things business-oriented. I certainly did anything I could to help budget-wise and labor-wise to implement her ideas for the young families. We started to do a midweek supper for the families to be able to have a night off cooking at home, and for these events I was the head cook and Miles the "chief bottle washer." A couple of the parents would always pitch in even though it was meant to give them a little relief. We knew to respect them enough to accept their help graciously.

Even though the rector took Christina's magnetic personality and substantial gifts in stride, once she had moved on to her own parish in Texas, I sensed the little bit of wind the rector had in his sails was gone. Soon he was looking for another job and got one as chaplain at a large religious retirement complex. I did think this was probably a good fit for him. His wife was a librarian, and she found a part-time job which was all she really wanted anyway. They left Boone, and I found myself treasurer, worship organizer and leader for the next year while we looked for another priest.

Neither Miles nor I were on the search committee, but Miles was on the vestry and I was, of course, ex officio as treasurer. New arrivals were briefed on the escapades going back to the terminated priest so as to fully understand the weight of their task. By the time they brought in their three final candidates, I had no qualms about their process and due diligence, and few qualms about the actual candidates. We didn't have the congregational polity where the entire church votes, so it was left ultimately to the bishop, the "canon to the ordinary" (or boom-boom as Miles referred to him) and the vestry—Miles being a voting member and me not. By now, we were on our third bishop since our arrival—one who, it seemed to us, spent more time looking in the mirror dressed in his vestments than shepherding his flock.

Two months in, I felt like I was reliving the Hope Mennonite minister days of my childhood. The priest's wonderful credentials and perfect references masked a peculiar mindset bent on the unfortunate political divide which was truly beginning to infect the entire country. I'm not sure he'd formulated enough thought on his true beliefs to know himself where he was on the spectrum. Still, this was no less problematic for me than the days with the Baton Rouge, Church of God minister. His largely incoherent yet dogmatic views were just as ugly, even if he was "all in" for same-gender marriage—or claimed to be. Neither of us ever believed him on that score.

His sermons were packed with words most would need a dictionary to unpack, which we assumed was supposed to impress us with his intellect. People seemed to love him or hate him. He had little interest in children or youth, and it showed quickly enough that the spurt of growth Christina had brought in and nurtured was quickly squandered and gone.

A wonderful couple whose two boys we'd known, who grew up in our time there, had both joined the Marines; and he was so judgmental about their doing so, the couple left out of complete alienation—as did another couple who were good friends of theirs. He had no discernment for recognizing the gifts of the laity. Soon, after his "all in" conversation with us, he gave a woman who was "all against" inclusion the role of heading up ministry to children and youth. This seemed to be a pattern of his leadership—if you can call it that. Stirring things up appeared to be his favorite pastime.

Miles summed up our take saying, "Take an ego, give it some authority, pile on intellectual superiority and this is what you get. There is nothing worse than listening to an intelligent person articulate a stupid idea."

I said, "As you'll recall from my Hope Mennonite minister days, you can't make a 'read' of humility when they are under authority, where they have to look good. It's only when they are moved out from under that, you see the real deal. I think he may have multiple personality disorder."

I knew he didn't. If he had, I could have been more sympathetic to his peculiarities.

It was the beginning of the end for us. By the time word got around that we had a Massachusetts marriage license, the division in the church was so rigid no one could see straight. But Miles and I could see one thing clearly—our way straight out the door. After a certain age, one loses the notion of seeking others' approval for one's life. We had reached that age. We were just glad our closest friends were gone by then and didn't have to see it unfold as it did.

I made my best attempt at reconciliation with the "all against crowd" and their cheerleader—the woman in charge of educating the young on Christianity—to no avail. I was less concerned about Miles and myself, and more concerned about the young boys and girls of another generation who would again face alienation from their church as so many before have faced. Once driven from their community of faith, they would then be labeled as godless and lost.

All this made me reflect on what might have been below the surface back in my Hope Mennonite days. While my parents knew and accepted Miles as part of the family, they were both dead before he and I married. I'm not sure how they might have responded to that. In my childhood and adolescent years, inclusion of "our kind" was not discussed one way or the other. Hope

Mennonite certainly had a number of men and women who never married and were never questioned as to why that might be. In one case, two older women lived together all their adult life, and no gossip was ever circulated about them. All these men and women were faithful members, accepted without reservation or snickering behind their back.

Sadly, this would all change one day as the country divided itself along political lines rather than the grace-filled life that had informed the generations before me.

Chapter Thirty-seven

Leaving church in this way also took me back to a day at the university when a young man, Ollie Elliot, in the physical plant asked if he could talk to me about a personal matter. There's not much you can say to that other than "yes," though one always enters such conversations with at least a twinge of apprehension—at least I always did, living with another man and most of my world knowing it.

As it turns out, he was struggling with his own identity and had overheard a zealot at the university using the line his church espoused, "Love the sinner and hate the sin."

He said, "I heard what he said to you and it didn't seem to faze you in the least, which prompted him to go off and talk about your lost soul. Are you a lost soul?"

I said, "Before I answer that, I've always wanted to tell you—I think you have the best name ever. I just love saying, 'Ollie Elliot.'"

"You and my mother," he said. "She loved to holler up the stairs to get me up in the morning, 'Ollie Elliot! Ollie Elliot!' She sounded like a parrot. I thought it was a goofy name, but I'm beginning to appreciate it for its uniqueness."

Getting to his question I asked him, "Ollie Elliot, are you really asking me, is your soul in peril for the same reason he asserts mine is lost? Are you struggling with this yourself?"

"Yes, I am, though I've never talked to anyone about it, and I have done everything I can to repress my feelings," Ollie responded.

"I'm glad you used the word 'repress,'" I said. "But before I explain why I'm glad you chose that word, I'd first like to say something about 'loving the sinner and hating the sin.' I have had a total of four people use that line on me in my life, and in all four cases it simply wasn't the reality of their conviction. They did not hate the sin—they were obsessed with the sin. And that obsession was a barrier to any chance that they could know how to love me and other beings in their 'hate the sin' category. I suppose it is possible some do better in this regard than others. All I can do is speak from experience, and it has been absolutely the case in all four persons, they were both obsessed with 'my sin' and incapable of showing any love towards me.

"What you should understand about the man you overheard is this—he is a crusader in the 'Church of All Certainty.' He and his church have all the answers, having failed to entertain any inconvenient questions. The extreme examples of these become the protestors outside complete strangers' funerals where they hold up signs that the dead boy is in hell and god—small 'g' god for their god is small and narrow—and 'god hates fags.'

"In the 'Church of All Certainty,' you must check your mind at the door and accept portions of the Bible—like juicy parts of Leviticus and subservient texts like Timothy—to define your worldview. The problem is, they don't seem to know the difference between resisting temptation and repression. They ask of you to resist the choice of your lifestyle when you know, as you have said, you are being asked to repress your very being.

"Repression never ends well. It will drive one mad or miserable or both. It is apt to inflict that misery not only on oneself but on others unintentionally—for example, marrying when you shouldn't, or being estranged from people you love or want to love when you shouldn't have to be estranged. I dare say in the most problematic and repressed mind, it leads to perversions and psychosis and self-destruction and suicide. Repression is violence against the self, it seems to me.

"There are, of course, many prevalent diabolical behaviors having nothing to do with repression—some, our society seems to actually reward, and some we lock up and throw away the key—but that's another subject altogether.

"Sin, my dear Ollie Elliot, isn't failing to repress, it is failing to love—to love God, ourselves and others. You can begin to see how resisting temptation is something we must strive for, and when we fail we must begin again and again and again—being reborn in the most dynamic sense of the term. We are tempted to make short cuts that are poor stewardship of the world. This is not loving God. We are tempted to deprive ourselves of simple joys in some twisted quest for piety and purity. This is not loving ourselves. We are tempted to lash out at others in anger, or seek momentary pleasure from them in heated passion that is bound to hurt others—adultery being one form of this. This is not loving others. Any kind of intimacy can fall prey to this as it is pretty well impossible to know the mind of the other. The best we can do is try to love, and seek forgiveness and reconciliation when we fail and hurt others.

"There are plenty of times I dread facing again another zealot crusader from the 'Church of All Certainty,' but I don't see them going away anytime soon—despite all my prayers for their blindness to the Gospel message of love and non-judgment.

"I would say the worst thing *you* can do is give yourself over to a life of repression. Celebrate who you are, even if it is quietly as I have done most of my life with those closest to me. Living a life in love is the great blessing of humanity—to ourselves and our world. Don't let some zealot rob you of that. Don't let them tell you their love is somehow good and your love is bad. That is just another form of bigotry which projects their superiority over you. This is exactly what the crusader was saying as he proclaimed his 'love the sinner and hate the sin' when confronting me with his 'truth.'

"I have found a way to get them to leave me alone. It doesn't come with any guarantees, however—and I hope it would never bring the kind of rage that ends in violence. On that front, I have been most fortunate—never encountering fists in my face or feet kicking the shit out of me. Though I am not so naive as to think it couldn't still happen one day. What I do is lift my right arm, make the sign of the cross and say, 'The Lord bless and keep you.' Sometimes this has been in actual practice, and sometimes only as a prayer for them in my mind as I stand facing them. Somehow they leave me alone after that—going off as our crusading brother did and telling others of my lost soul.

"A deer's grace and beauty doesn't come by repressing its being. So too our grace and beauty comes from within—from our very being." I smiled and asked, "What do you make of all that, Ollie Elliot?"

He smiled back and said, "I think I need to start dating. It's time to get on with my life."

"Good," was all I said.

As I told Miles about this a few weeks later I said, "His countenance has truly lightened and the crusader has lost all his power over young Ollie Elliot."

159

"Good," Miles said, adding, "You do like that name, don't you —Ollie Elliot?"

I answered, "Can't help but notice you worked it into your question. You like it too."

He said, "It is a cute name."

Ollie did find love and, in time, a more or less accepting family —more or less it seems is about as good as one can hope for. Miles and I might have finally been able to have some younger friends, but they moved out of state to get a fresh start. He is good about keeping in touch by email—letting me know the joys and challenges of their lives.

It seems so strange to reduce friendships of more than two decades to a few pages. The truth is, these were years of simple, joyous routine interrupted along the way by troublesome clergy and their loyal followers. There was little drama from day-to-day and because of our friends' ages and empty nests, not even much interaction beyond our close-knit group.

I took as an article of faith the children's song we'd sung at Hope Mennonite—

Jesus loves the little children.
All the Children of the world.
Red, and yellow, black and white,
they are precious in his sight.
Jesus loves the little children of the world.

Perhaps it was this simple article of faith that allowed me to feel genuine affection, and no fear or feeling of superiority, for Louie, CJ, Darnell and Gloria back in Baton Rouge. And perhaps they looked at the young, white man with some hope in their heart that change was possible.

While our Episcopalian friends in Boone were sensitive enough not to express openly racist attitudes, Miles and I always sensed something when any "minorities" were around. It's a terrible thing to say, but I felt like they would be glad to have them clean for them, or mow for them—but the notion of spending an evening or Derby day together seemed like altogether an impossibility.

I couldn't cast the stone as it must be said. Poorer blacks, browns and whites cleaned the buildings on campus and mowed the lawns. None were ever invited by me to dinner. After my one semester in the college cafeteria, I made sure they were never invisible—only to be applauded for making a mess. For the ones I knew at all, I got them something every Christmas to say thank you. A few times each year I would stay up all night making my mom's cinnamon rolls so I could have them there when the custodial staff came into work at 5:00 AM. I would have been glad to try for better, but I had the feeling—as I'd had when others would come up to my work companions in Baton Rouge—that their subservient personalities were never fully suppressed and my kindness, while clearly appreciated, shouldn't suggest they'd let down their guard too easily.

With our friends all dead or moved away, and our life now cut off from our church family, I said to Miles, "Maybe we should visit a black church. At least the singing would be good and the preaching, if a bit long for our taste, would be more exciting than we'd been used to getting of late."

I said this in all seriousness, but our own fears surfaced when we wondered how such a church would look at two aging, white men, wearing matching wedding bands. And so, until the spirit would move otherwise, we decided to spend our days in greater seclusion.

Building House and Home

Chapter Thirty-eight

Miles never knew very many old French Cajun sayings. A few he understood but rarely used. One he used with great frequency was "Pauvre bête," which in its literal French means "poor animal," but is used by the Cajuns to say, "Poor thing." Any complaint I might have about work or church or him met with the same unsympathetic response, "Pauvre bête!"

I'd fuss at him with one of my mother's lines, "Oh für die Liebe der Schweizer." It seemed to serve as Mom and Grandma's substitution for swearing—instead of saying, "Oh, for the love of God," their version was "Oh, for the love of the Swiss." It is one of those things Mom said, but I don't believe she knew herself what it meant. Not knowing any German, neither did Miles—and I pretended I did but wouldn't say. I did figure it out and only confessed to him the meaning on one of our trips to Switzerland.

The other expression he would use with urgency was "*Allons!*": "get a move on it." Or he'd use it more frequently as simply, "Allons,": "let's go."

Travis and Winston had really been godsends to us. For the first time ever, we finally had two friends with whom we could talk about anything without any reservation. They too were more relaxed with us than they'd ever been with their two old bridge partners who spent the evening bickering.

We drove them one Sunday afternoon to see a lot we had our eye on and where we hoped to build. Travis loved little home projects—inside or out. Winston, as it turns out, kept his hands busy doing needlepoint (when one hand wasn't holding a cigarette), and in addition to all the pieces hanging in their house, he had also organized a group of women at the church to do kneelers for the communion rail. I laid out the house plans I'd done on the hood of the car which Travis could already picture completed.

Winston took one look at the plans and said, "Honey, I can't feature how nothin' looks with anything till I sees it together."

Miles said, "I guess we oughta be seein' if da oil be needin' checkin,'" and we loaded back in the car and went to Kentucky Fried Chicken for lunch.

We bought the two-acre plot and hired the needed contractors to get our new timber frame home started. We were sure to sequence things so the side of the duplex we planned to live in was always a step ahead of the rental side. I used my first year's vacation days—taking each Friday off during times when I could work on the duplex, and Miles did the same. What he lacked in carpenter skills, he made up for in another set of hands and a strong back.

One Saturday, a man pulled up in an old pickup that looked like it had been sitting in a chicken coop for fifteen years. It was covered in bird shit and dust. He had a rope to hold the driver's side door shut. He wandered up to where we were working on the roof.

I looked down and said, "Can I help you?"

No response. He just continued to stare up at us. Miles pulled up another of his much less frequently used Cajun sayings mumbling, "Il est pas tô la."

I knew it meant the guy "wasn't all there" and hoped he wasn't from south Louisiana. If he did understand Miles, it didn't faze him. He just stood there, and I thought the best course might just be to carry on with our work.

Finally he spoke, "Ahhh, I-I wasa wondering if you was wanting some help."

"No, I'm sorry. We're doing the work ourselves."

He didn't respond but stood there a minute more staring and walked back to his truck.

Miles said, "I hope he wasn't casing the joint."

I responded, "If we was, he certainly gave us plenty of time to give the police a description of him and his truck."

Then I said, "I hope he wasn't Jesus seeing if we'd be hospitable to him. It reminds me of a story told of my great-grandmother Schudel. During the depression there were lots of men—hobos as my grandma passed down the story—who would stop in at farms for a meal. Great-grandma always fed them. It was believed that somehow they marked the farms where they were welcomed so

163

that others coming along would know they'd get fed. One man asked if she had a bed for him to sleep that night. She apologized and said she didn't have a room. She heard him say as he went out the gate and back to the road, 'No room, no room; will there be room enough in heaven for me?' After that, my great-grandma always kept a bedroom ready."

Miles said, "If that was supposed to make me feel guilty for accusing him of casing the joint it worked. But I'd still say, Il est pas tô la."

"I don't think he *was* all there," I acknowledged. "I thought he might at least ask for some gas or food money which I would have given him. If he ever shows up again, I might find some little something he could do just to see if he actually can follow instructions."

We never saw him again. If he *was* Jesus, we had failed him once more.

We did all the roofing, setting the windows, trim work, staining, siding, masonry accents and so forth. Miles said from the get-go, "I don't want a single board of sheetrock in the house."

The ceilings and walls inside were all tongue and groove pine stained with a light hazelnut, low-gloss finish we'd found through a log home stain company. The outside was cedar siding and native rock. The rock work was the slowest going. I knew how to do it, but I didn't have the natural gift for eyeing just the right stone for the right spot and so some trial and error was required.

A few times I got pretty frustrated and said to Miles, "There must be a good Cajun word I could use when I'm ready to throw my trowel across the yard."

He responded, "There is, but you won't let me use such language. It's a universally understood word starting with 'f'."

"You're no help," I said.

Even though I'd watched my uncles build fireplaces, I wasn't keen on burning down our new house, so I did want to bring in a skilled mason to lay up the fireplaces for the two apartments. I'd asked around the physical plant and one of our tradesmen, Isaiah, said I should come with him that afternoon to take a look at his daddy's work. The crew consisted of his dad, Micah, who was in his sixties and Isaiah's older brother, Jeremiah, who worked with him. They tended for each other, only dragging in other help if needed for some reason which, according to Isaiah, usually meant him working on Saturday.

I said, "You sure are a prophetic family! Do you have a brother Amos too?"

He laughed and said, "No, but I do have one named Ezekiel."

I was curious, "What names do the girls get?"

"Esther, Ruth, Sarah and Rebekah," he answered.

"I guess I don't have to ask if your family are churchgoing folk," I said.

He answered, "My grandpa was a mason by trade and the minister at the AME church in town by vocation—unpaid for thirty-five years."

We left work a few minutes early, and I followed him over to a job where they were working. They were just finishing up for the day. One look at his daddy and I immediately thought of Louie. He had the same muscular build and pleasant smile—but no gold and diamond tooth that I could spot at least. I didn't have to study their work long. I could see right away they had the gift, and the fireplace they were working on was exactly what I wanted.

I said, "I guess I don't have to sketch out what I want—this is exactly what I want. If you're interested, I'd sure like you to come build two just like this for my duplex."

Micah said, "Isaiah has told us you're a good man. We could start in three weeks if that works for you."

"Isaiah's a good man, and I can see it comes to him honestly." Confirming the plan I said, "Three weeks should work out just right."

When I got home and told Miles he said, "Well, what's it gonna cost?"

I confessed, "I never asked."

"You hired men to build two rock fireplaces and never asked," he said in some dismay. "Did we come into money I don't know about?"

I offered some reassurance, "I had built into the construction loan ample budget for two rock fireplaces. I don't have the slightest inkling that we're going to get ripped off by them."

To that he said, "You'd better hope not!"

Their actual, final bill was $1,500 under my estimate. I never told Miles that and paid them my budgeted amount. Micah didn't want to take it, but I said, "You got over here as promised and did the work as promised. Just think of it as returning gratitude for gratitude."

They were going to be back the next day to load up their scaffolding, mixer and such. Jeremiah said, "Well, at least let us lay up two nice mailbox columns for you before we take off."

I had already poured two small footers as I'd plan to build my own, and they'd obviously spotted them.

"You trying to make a grown man cry?" I asked.

They both just laughed at that, and Micah said, "Be back in the morning."

We kept two lawn chairs at the construction site for us to sit in when taking breaks. That evening we hauled them into the living room of our apartment and sat looking at the fine rockwork next to those beautiful timbers and the hammer beam trusses. We ate our hamburgers and chocolate malts staring and not saying a word.

Finally Miles said, "Prettiest fireplace I've ever seen. I don't even care if it went over budget. I never pictured it looking like that."

All I said was, grinning to myself just a bit, "Right on budget."

"Wonderful," he said.

Chapter Thirty-nine

With the good contacts I had from the university and some I got from Bill Cross, we really were fortunate. The build went smoothly and was consistently on or slightly under budget. Bill, who soon after our arrival in Boone had offered me a project manager job about an hour too late, didn't work with timber frames and so passed on building our place. His two boys, John and Ansel, ran the best building supply and hardware store in town. Ansel was more back of the house and John was always out front. They were well respected for the excellent service they provided, and if they didn't have what you were looking for, John would have Ansel "search the wide earth," as he put it, to find it.

Now, I was giving them some of my own business as well as plenty of business through my work at the university. John and I got well acquainted. Anytime we'd see each other at a restaurant, we tended to join whichever one was already there. Since he'd often find Miles and me at the Daisy Cafe for breakfast, this almost became our regular social club.

When John first decided to run for city council, I even took up the most active political role of my life—serving as his campaign manager. I'm not sure he needed one given his standing in the community, but he asked me if I would, and so I did.

I never attended any weddings or funerals in their family, but somehow we had a comfortable relationship that afforded us a high level of trust between each other. As far as I could ascertain, integrity was a core value of the Cross family and wouldn't be short-changed for a quick profit.

John's sister and brother-in-law owned a cabinet shop right next to the building supply. I doubted I'd do better on price or quality than having them do the cabinetry and countertops. I asked John about it.

He said, "I can give you a total of three names in town that I'd say could do a fine job for you. They would be one of the three. I won't recommend one over the other."

I said, "Does your sister know your egalitarian recommendations are costing her business?"

He laughed and said, "She does, and knows her own daddy does the same."

"She'll get my business if they can fit us in," I said. "I don't see any point not giving the Cross family first right of refusal."

To which he said, "Tell her I said you get the family price. See what she says to that."

He didn't elaborate, but I did as instructed. His sister laughed and said, "When I go to the lumber yard, John says my markup is 10% over the listed price for being a nuisance."

"Sounds like something a brother would tell his sister," I chuckled.

"I'm nicer than he is," she replied. "I'll give you 10% off."

I asked her why they never bid on university work, and I very much respected her answer.

"We've always had all the work we can handle, and have no interest in expanding to some big shop that is more headaches than it's worth. We're content to make a living and don't need to make a killing."

"You are a Cross," I said.

The kitchen and bath cabinets, and other built-ins and bookcases were as beautiful as the rock fireplace and the timber frame joinery. It's not a stretch to say their work was exquisite. I said to Miles, "I can't believe the quality of workmanship we've lucked into on this place."

He said, "People's jaws are going to drop when they walk in here. Mine still does every time."

Late October we got the few pieces of furniture we'd need to move in lined up so they could be delivered when our apartment was finished. We moved in one week before Christmas, put up the Christmas tree and had Winston and Travis, Ellery and Nan, and Miles' co-worker Madi and her husband over for our own little mini-open house.

The house was plenty of Christmas present to ourselves already, but we wanted one other to go with it. We'd lined up getting two golden retriever pups which were weaned and ready for us to come get. Our first house guests were greeted by two bundles of golden fur, named Jem and Scout.

I told my guests, "Once they know their names I want to go to the back door and call out, 'Jem, Scout, come on in,' just like Atticus Finch."

Winston said, "You are too easily amused. I guess you'll start calling Miles, Calpurnia, and expect him to cook and cleanup."

I said, "I might just do that. I just hope Jem doesn't expect me to play football for the Methodists."

Madi had no idea what any of this was about, but decided she'd ask Miles about it at work. She asked her husband on the ride home, and he didn't know either.

Miles told her, "*To Kill a Mockingbird* is one of our favorite movies—and books. Watch the movie, and it will all make sense." He wanted her to see it rather than just explain bits and pieces.

She clearly had watched it when she said to Miles one Monday morning, "Don't start calling me Ms. Maudie. As close as that sounds to Madi, I'm surprised you call me by my right name. But if you do call me Ms. Maudie, I'll just call you Bob Ewell."

Miles said, "Damn, I'd be getting the worst part of that deal! I'd rather be Boo Radley. Then you could say, 'Hey, Boo.'"

Recalling the day back in Brown County when we saw the young man's golden take off and dive into the water, we were eager for summer to come so we could take the dogs with us camping up on Watauga Lake. It didn't go exactly as planned. When we took Jem and Scout to the water's edge, there was no great leap into the lake. We tugged them towards the beach and both acted like we were crazy trying to get them wet. We got into the lake ourselves, as we had planned to do to cool off anyway, and coaxed them in. Jem finally waded in and was quickly over his head as I moved back encouraging him forward. His ass-end was sinking and nose not far from going under with the rest of him.

Miles hollered out, "He's drowning!"

I said, "Surely he'll start paddling out of instinct."

He never did with force enough to bring himself back up to the surface, so I moved to him to scoop him up into my arms. Scout was no better and never would even wade in far enough to get in over her head. Our swimming-with-our-dogs-fantasy—having them retrieve sticks (or ducks) for us—was deflated completely.

The retrieval-of-water-fowl instinct skipped a generation or something. We had adorable water dogs who hated the water.

This was a trait to be shared later with what might have been more expected from our cattle-dog, red heeler-mixed mutts, Bonnie and Penny. They were one notch worse on the scale. If you got them within three feet of any water, they would put their front paws out, spread as wide as possible with claws extended, legs stiff as boards—putting the brakes on so as to go not an inch further. In their case seeing this was pretty amusing.

Penny always liked being high up on things. Her one exception to the no-water rule was when she saw a rock protruding out of a small stream. She looked at it a moment and went skipping across the few feet of flowing water to be up on that rock to have a look around. I guess the view wasn't any better. When I'd take her to the same spot on other outings she'd just ignore it. "Been there, done that," I guess was her reckoning.

The goldens we had in between Jem and Scout and Bonnie and Penny were true to their nature. Rudy and Rusty loved the water and would plop in it even if it was not much more than a mud puddle. They could not only swim but both liked to dive—especially Rudy. He'd be under so long, sometimes we'd wondered if he was going to come up alive. When he finally would, he'd never come up "empty-handed." He'd have the root of one of the cottonwoods or willows that grew nearby in his mouth—which might still be attached as he would back out of the water, tugging as he went until he finally would break a piece of it loose. He had all the patience in the world for these endeavors. He'd chew on it a while and be back in the water to dive for more. Rusty was less patient and stuck to quick head-bobs underwater to get whatever rock he might be able to drag out.

Both would paddle after ducks or geese, swimming with them in the water, and only turn around when they decided the pursuit wasn't going to end with a bird to bring back to shore. They could spot any stick we threw and paddle out and bring it back to us.

Chapter Forty

The summer after we moved in, Miles' dad, Frankie, decided he wanted to escape some of the Louisiana summer and came to spend two weeks with us. I had never visited with him more than an hour here or there, and when we went to Franklin for visits we always stayed at a motel at my insistence so as not to impose. He decided to fly up, and we picked him up in Charlotte. He had retired recently, and was still adjusting as to what to do with himself day-to-day. He never really knew how to strike up a conversation with Miles, and Miles was no better at it than he. I had a general notion, if we were going to converse much, I'd probably have to take the lead—which is not exactly one of my gifts. I did think at least I'd be inclined to greater effort than Miles. And I was curious to know more about him and his roots, as Miles didn't seem to know much beyond the fact they were Cajun.

Frankie said his dad was sheriff of St. Mary Parish for most all Frankie's adult life. That much I knew, and I knew it also was one of the roots of Miles' angst regarding Louisiana justice and his own family's complicity in its complicated history. Frankie didn't get any further before it reminded him of a story that Miles had not heard before.

"I had a brother who was a state trooper and my cousin a city cop in Franklin," Frankie started out. "An old, mulatto Cajun truck driver came barrell-assin' into town with his engine brake cranking down that diesel engine, and rear-ended daddy's sheriff's car with daddy in it. Daddy's nephew was soon there with his lights flashing as he pulled up in his city cop car. The old trucker was already a nervous wreck—and my cousin was being a shit-ass, it must be said, giving him as hard a time as possible. The trucker saw both men's name was Bergeron. When a state trooper pulled up, the trucker went running back to him and said, "You gotta help me. These Bergerons are giving me a hard time."

My brother said, "And I'm a Bergeron too, and that's my daddy's car you ran up on."

The old trucker put both hands on the side of his head and said, "Oh, mon Dieu, I'm havin' a bad day."

Miles, expressing some deep-seated suspicion of their character said, "I'll bet they made sure he spent at least one night in jail just because they could."

I said, "That's not a very nice thing to say about your kinfolk."

"Well, actually he is right," Frankie said.

To which Miles said, "Them's my peeps."

Frankie didn't know the family going back much more than his grandparents. So far as he knew they were all transplants from France to Acadia to Louisiana.

Up to his arrival, we had continued work on the other side of the duplex and had it done when he arrived. Still, we had no furniture in it nor any money set aside to buy any. He stayed with us in our half. We hadn't had any time to start in earnest on the yard and garden. He liked working in the dirt and was eager to help. We all went to the nursery together and ended up making multiple trips as we bought plants and placed them, laying things out as we went, with no particular plan in mind. He had a good eye for layering things just so, and I trusted his instinct. In truth, he did most of the work. I offered to rent a tiller, but he insisted on hand digging. While we were at work he was working out front and in back to get things in the ground.

As I both congratulated him and thanked him for all the wonderful work he'd done he said, "I'm sure you've heard Miles talk about how much he and his brothers helped me in the garden."

Miles just stood there silent. "No, I'd not heard him talk about any love of gardening," I said.

Frankie said, "I always thought the only reason his brothers had to be in every sport at school was to be sure they didn't have to help me in the garden. And since Miles didn't like sports he had to look for every musical and play to be in. I did have to admit, though, he had a lot more talent for what he was doing than those brothers of his did in any sport."

Miles said to his dad, "I was about to say, 'Pauvre bête,' and then you go and say something nice like that."

Frankie laughed at that. "Now you sound like your mother. I'd come in fussin' about not having any help from you boys in the garden or washing the cars, and she'd say, 'Oh! Pauvre bête.' And then she'd add, 'You see how much help I get in here.'"

Miles clarified the record a bit, "I did finally take over the car washing."

Frankie clarified it further. "Only after you had your driver's license and you could drive through the auto-washer."

"Well," was all Miles could say to that.

I don't know what made me think of it, but I recalled my childhood, hog-riding stories and how my dad had put a stop to it.

Frankie thought that was the funniest thing. "If we'd have been out on a farm instead of in town, I bet me and my brothers could have done some good hog ridin'. I guess I'm too big and too old to take it up now. C'est la vie."

We asked if he wanted to stay an extra week or so, and he decided if we'd have him he would. He just hoped the boys back home were watering the garden as they said they would. We suggested we take the extra time it gave us and take a two-day trip down to Asheville to see Biltmore.

"I don't know what it is," he said, "But if that's something you want to do, I'll ride along. Seems like a ways to drive to look at an old house."

He didn't seem impressed with Miles trying to explain it to him but didn't have any objection to going. We had seen it on our first trip to North Carolina when we'd gone to escape some of the Baton Rouge summer.

When we arrived, it is best stated that we enjoyed it for a second time as much as we had the first, but the better word for Frankie was mesmerized. He would look up and turn his head back and forth, jaw dropped open, hardly ever saying a word.

The only thing he would say is, "Lordie-lordie."

At dinner that night he smiled, and said in his most pitiful voice, "That Mr. Vanderbilt—pauvre bête."

When we got back to the apartment, we had a big storm rumble through. It knocked out the electricity and stayed off for several hours. We all wished the ceiling fans were on as it was a warm, still night. As bedtime approached and we thought how much more comfortable sleep would be with a little air movement, Frankie stood up, raised both arms, palms up and said, "Let there be light."

No light and no fans.

He looked at Miles and said, "I guess I'm not God—if you had any lingering doubts, now you know."

Miles smiled at him and said, "Pauvre bête."

When the light and fans came on a minute later, I said to Frankie, "You may not be God, but you must have a good connection."

And he said, "I can live with that."

As we were driving back from Charlotte after seeing his dad off, Miles said, "I never thought I'd describe three weeks with my dad as delightful, but it truly was. The key must be to get him by himself away from my brothers."

I said, "To hear him talk about your brothers and their parade of wives and troublesome children, I'd say he's relieved to have one happy, well-adjusted son with no prospect of more grandchildren—even if he does live with another man."

Miles said, "Amazing, wasn't it? He just acted as though hanging with us was as comfortable as he and Mom sitting at home watching TV."

"Why do you say that like you're about to cry?" I asked.

"Because I am," he said.

We drove the rest of the way back to Boone in silence.

Chapter Forty-one

That was the one and only trip Frankie ever made to North Carolina. It prompted Miles to be a lot better about calling his dad every week or two, and it seemed to open up both men to be able to talk to the other. Miles would tell him about what we were up to—skipping Miles' work talk as Frankie never understood exactly what Miles did. His dad would tell him how the garden was doing and what his "couillon brothers" were up to, which was never good. He wondered about coming up in the fall after the garden was done—he hadn't been too pleased with the boys tending the garden on his last visit. It would have been just over two years since his last trip.

One August morning that summer, he was out in the garden and collapsed. His neighbor was in his backyard and heard just a single moan. He went to look over their common fence and saw Frankie lying on the ground, not moving. He called to him and got no response. He went in and phoned 911, and headed over to wait for the ambulance. By the time they arrived he was confirmed dead. "Massive heart attack—dead before he hit the ground," the coroner said.

By now Robert, Miles' coworker and our friend, was living in the duplex next door, and he volunteered to take care of Jem and Scout while we were gone. We quickly accepted his offer and decided to drive rather than fly. We were in Franklin the next morning, had breakfast and went straight on to the funeral home. No one from the family was there yet. They led us into the parlor where his dad was laid. We both stood silent staring at the body, which only a few hours earlier was still making plans for its future.

"Do you want to go to the house and see who's over there?" I asked.

"No," Miles said. "We'll just sit here with Dad."

The Catholic church in Franklin is a very nice church and, gratefully, the priest who led the service clearly knew Frankie and offered all the consolation and hope families need at such times of loss. Frankie was interred next to Bella in the Catholic cemetery, and we went back to the homeplace after it was all done. At the funeral home, funeral and now at the house I tried to work out who belonged to whom. Miles was little help. There were wives, ex-wives, children, stepchildren, and unknown neighbors. By then I'd at least figured out who the surviving aunts and uncles were, but wasn't sure what they knew about us. I decided the best course for me was to make my way into the backyard and be as invisible as possible.

A few did ask over the days, "How did you know Frankie?"

"I'm a friend of his youngest son, and met Frankie that way," I'd say. That way if they didn't know who Miles was, at least I didn't have to explain it any further. A couple of the ex-wives had figured out who I was and came up to talk to me. We actually had a nice visit, though it did humor me to think, "If you had any idea what I know about you, you'd be mortified." Frankie didn't hold back when it came to telling Miles and me all their "shenanigans" as he put it.

We weren't back home two weeks before I got an early morning call from my mom. "Your dad was up some time in the night and dropped dead just outside the bedroom. I didn't hear him get up or notice he was gone until I woke up this morning."

Men and heart attacks! There are worse ways to go, but Miles and I hadn't quite expected burying "the other father" this soon. We repeated the drill with Robert watching the dogs and us driving straight through, this time to northern Ohio. This would be Miles' first Mennonite funeral and our first trip back to the farm since our college days. There wouldn't be any motorcade from the church to the cemetery. The pallbearers would carry Dad from the church on the corner of the old Shudel farm to his grave on the corner of the old Kibler farm, interring him next to his oldest son, Wayne, already in the ground.

Mom, of course, wanted me and Miles to sing. She had two requests—*Jesus Paid It All* as we had sung at Park Place our last Sunday there and *Great Is Thy Faithfulness* as I had sung for Aunt Ilah all those years ago. We did as asked, which as I predicted, brought about the next request following the service.

"Boys, you know I expect the same when my time comes," she said as though no debate was possible—which in her mind was already an absolute given.

176

I said, "Could be we'll be too old to sing by then. You might live a long time."

Her comeback to that was, "I didn't say it had to be pretty. You can croak it out if you have to, but I suspect you'll not be that far gone when my time is up."

Whether she was going by instinct, some premonition of a distinct outcome, some diagnosis or "just supposin'," I can't say. What I can say is, we got a call just over a year later from her when she announced, "Looks like I'm done for. Doc says I've got cancer everywhere."

I was planning to call her later that day to see if she would be up for a trip with us to Switzerland. We'd talked about it a couple times but never got around to doing anything about it. Now it looked like we'd waited too long.

I didn't know what to say. What came out was, "Were you as surprised by the doctor's news as I am by your news, or did you already know?"

All she said was, "I guess it's a surprise even when you know."

"We'll be up to see you soon." And with that we said goodbye.

Thank goodness for Robert next door. Not only was he a good friend and a good colleague of Miles, he was number one dependable when we needed his help as we did yet again.

Miles and I decided we'd see what the prognosis was once we got there as to what my plans should be. I could get leave time if I needed it to help care for her. I already knew she was an advocate for hospice, so I couldn't imagine she would have any fuss about bringing them in. She would want to die at home—that much I was sure about.

She had a house full of visitors when we arrived, including a quartet from Hope Mennonite which was singing in the bedroom where she was lying.

That evening when it was just us kids, she gave her latest update from the doctor's visit that morning. "He gives me two weeks."

That was a bit of a shock, but I did think if it were me, I'd rather go quicker than lingering for months on end. As it went, two weeks became four weeks, then six weeks passed. She said to me one evening, "I'm supposed to be dead by now. Why am I still here?"

I said, "Because that doctor doesn't know what a tough old bird you are."

She said, "Well the old bird ain't too tough anymore. Someone meaning well said she was praying for me to get better. I felt like punching her—not very Mennonite of me. I don't want to go through this again. I'm ready to go."

"I know you are," I said.

"You haven't forgotten—you and Miles have to sing at my funeral."

"Did we promise that?" I asked.

"You weren't asked; you were told," she said and a minute later was asleep.

Over those six weeks I was able to go back and forth every other week, help my sisters with home care and be there for the many hospice visits. Mom had lots of visits from neighbors, relatives and old classmates. She had two tables set up with a bunch of personal things. She'd tell her guests to pick something if they wanted a keepsake. She liked clocks and had one to give her remaining children and grandchildren. My sisters didn't like her cuckoo clock. I loved it! It had been handed down to her from Grandma Shudel. It was both cuckoo and music box and looked like a Swiss chalet.

I remembered too on those New Year's Eve celebrations at our house how the cuckoo was the official countdown clock—and how as we hollered, "Happy New Year," the cuckoo would count its twelve "cuckoos" and then play its little Swiss folk tune on the music box.

Mom died on one of my weeks back in Boone. I talked to her on the phone just moments before she died—well that is to say, I said goodbye and that I loved her. She was too weak and her breathing too labored to respond. Minutes later came the call—she was gone.

Chapter Forty-two

With the settlement of the Bergeron and Kibler estates, we didn't inherit a whole lot. We had always paid extra on our mortgage and, with one car and not a whole lot of driving, we weren't spending much on transportation. We put what we did get from the estates on the mortgage and had it all but paid off. This we thought would be key to allowing us to retire early if we wanted to go that route.

Miles and I were both now "orphans"—parents and grandparents all gone. None had really lived well into old age even though all had died of "natural causes"—and Miles' mom made it barely past middle age. War had taken the only one from our generation thus far and, except for the usual ailments of advancing age, all were in relative good health. Some of that relativity was weighted towards management by the pharmaceutical industry—including Miles.

Mom and Dad were always more inclined to regular check-ups than I was. I hadn't been to the doctor since I left to go to college. I knew I'd gotten too overweight, but I didn't see how I needed a doctor to tell me that. They told Miles plenty of times, and it didn't seem to be falling off him even as he ate more of what they told him to eat and less of what he liked. It was working out well for them. He made more and more frequent appointments as they were always wanting to adjust his medications. The new diet was offset also by side effects of some of the drugs, with weight gain as one of their main ones.

He had a blood pressure monitor that I would use every now and then, so I knew I was okay on that front. I even pricked my finger a few times to check my blood sugar, and knew I was trending right behind him of becoming a full-blown diabetic. All that was a very slow progression for us both. We spent many years drinking what we wanted, and eating what we wanted, and always felt energetic, healthy and happy.

In our working days we ate out more than in. We often skipped breakfast, and I would go to the Daisy Cafe most weekdays for lunch, hitting the Indian Buffet at least once a week. Miles, Madi and Robert switched mostly between a burger place, a Mexican restaurant and the Indian Buffet. We tried to go early on Saturdays for breakfast at the Daisy Cafe but, in time, resigned ourselves to the notion it was just easier to fix breakfast at home rather than deal with the weekend mayhem.

Sundays were reserved for lunch after church at the Highland Place Bistro. We were treated like royalty. The same table was always reserved for us. We left it as a standing reservation—letting them know if for some reason we wouldn't be there the next week. About the only reasons were times we were on vacation or at the country club with Ellery and Nan. The same waiter served us, though all the servers knew us and would be well informed of all our preferences if our usual waiter was out. Every few months before we would hear the specials, we'd be told, "The chef would like to make you something special today if you are agreeable." We were *always* agreeable. This would be something of his own creation not offered on the menu or as a special. Once it was Venison with a Madeira demi-glace. When the kitchen discovered they were out of raspberries, which we often had for a simple dessert after our delicious meals, I saw our waiter literally running over to the nearby grocery store to get some.

We showed our appreciation, both in terms of genuine kindness and respect for all the staff, as well as healthy tips. Our waiter, who had figured out we were both university employees and not tycoons, said to us, "You don't need to do what you do for us every week."

I just smiled and said, "You make every trip here special, and we just give what we want out of gratitude."

It was our one real extravagance, and sadly they closed about the same time we parted ways with our Episcopal church. We never found any other Sunday regular spot that quite filled the same niche. With the exception of the Daisy Cafe, we never got even remotely acquainted with the waitstaff or managers at other restaurants. It seemed like we'd rarely see the same one more than a few times—and even though we were never stingy tippers, few seemed to remember us and try to seat us at their table.

Certainly, the Daisy was anything but extravagant, but we had great admiration for their reliability, consistency and friendliness. We never knew it to close for any reason other than their scheduled day off of Monday. Head cook and manager, Noel, had arrived from Guam a year or two before we first discovered it. I never met a worker like him! His primary help was from Ethel and Maggie who were joined at the hip. Both had started as dishwashers in larger restaurants and moved to waitstaff in each restaurant before landing at Daisy's. Maggie's husband Bob had cooked for the original Daisy who owned the cafe. Bob was quite a bit older than Maggie. She was reluctant to work in the same restaurant as her husband, but when Bob hired Ethel she quickly joined her friend.

She said to Ethel, "You tell Bob to back off if he starts snappin' at me, you hear?"

She said this in front of her husband.

Ethel grinned at Bob and said to Maggie, "You *know* I've got your back!"

Chapter Forty-three

All I knew about Maggie and Ethel's childhoods was, according to Maggie, "Ethel and I grew up together in the backwaters of Tennessee."

Ethel wouldn't even say that much. Neither were in any way reserved around Miles and me, and the fact that they'd never elaborate suggested to us not to pry into what might be a dark past both had worked to put behind them.

After our tenant and friend Robert had died and Miles and I had returned from his funeral in Charlotte, we sat down with our house-and-dog sitter, Ethel, and told her of the strange family we'd encountered. This led her, somehow, to want to open up about her own family.

She said, "Let me tell you about strange families. I know you've heard Maggie say we were from the backwaters of Tennessee. That is a very generous way of putting it, even if it doesn't sound like it would be.

"We've known each other our entire lives. That backwater was actually a very small religious community so disconnected from the world around it—literally back in the hollers—and so far off any main road no one happened in by accident. We all lived on little ramshackle farms and barely eked out a living. Poverty can be a good teacher, but in our case, poverty wasn't the worst of it.

"I had a twin sister named Edith. When we were just over six years old, Edith got terribly ill. She was taken to the church where Brother Sylvanus prayed—well, more like screamed—over Edith with people laying hands on her. You see, Brother Sylvanus and the community wouldn't allow anyone to go to the doctor. You birthed your children at home and took them to be prayed over if sick. If they happened to die—well, that was just God's will.

"As far as I ever knew, when someone died there was never an inquest of any kind. The church buried them in their own cemetery. We also never knew of any birth certificates, which Maggie and I had to deal with when we left. But that's getting ahead of the story.

"I don't know what Edith had, but praying didn't cure her and so 'God called her home.' I was devastated. She and I were like most twins. I felt like half of me had died with her. I didn't know to even ask my mother and father why no doctor was ever called. How could I? We didn't know what doctors were. We had no TV or radio—such things were the 'work of the Devil' was all we knew about them. We didn't even have electricity; we didn't go to public schools. I guess somehow on religious grounds, the community persuaded someone in authority in Tennessee to let us have our own private school. You can imagine the stellar education we received.

"Maggie lived just up the road towards the school so she would always walk with me. We let our other siblings walk ahead, and we always deliberately kept behind them enough to have our own time together going to and coming back from school. We didn't even have a female school teacher like most kids.

"Brother Sylvanus was preacher and teacher, and if he had a golden rule it was 'Let the woman learn in silence with all subjection. But I suffer not a woman to teach, nor to usurp authority over the man, but to be in silence.'

"I can't even tell you where that is in the Bible, but I still remember it word for word—it was beaten into us on a constant basis. My mother and Maggie's as well were treated just in this manner at home every bit as much as at church. If my mother ever had fifty cents of her own money to spend, I never saw it. I'm certain she didn't.

"There were those children who left the community. In those cases the father would bring the 'dedication certificate' of the child that had been issued by the church when the child was first brought there after their birth—where they were 'dedicated to the Lord.'

"Brother Sylvanus would then take the certificate and burn it in a small metal bucket in front of the congregation and declare, 'Them that are without God be judged. Put away from among yourselves that wicked person.'

"Or something like that. We heard the lines about subservient women so often we'll never forget it. People leaving and being 'forever cast out' was, sadly, all too rare. Usually when it did happen it was when a boy and girl would run off together. We never knew of a girl or two running off on their own.

"My father was never physically abusive to me or my mother, but he waded right into the Brother Sylvanus bullshit with both feet and liked doin' it. He treated the boys one way and me and my mother like slaves to whatever he wanted. It was no different over at Maggie's.

"When we were seventeen, we plotted our escape. At least the boys who left always had a little money. We girls had nothing. Maggie suggested we get the dedication certificates for two reasons.

"She said, 'It will make Brother Sylvanus powerfully mad not to be able to burn 'em, and we might need 'em to prove we were actually born.'

"We both knew where they were kept and agreed we'd grab them before leaving. I told her I had discovered a couple years earlier a little hidey-hole of cash in the barn that my father kept hidden. I was sure he didn't know any of us knew about it.

"Maggie said, 'Are you worried about stealing it?'

"I said I was only worried about him finding out it was gone before we had a chance to make a clean break, and he'd be coming after us. I wasn't worried about him going to the sheriff—that would be dealing with the world they wanted no part of.

"We settled on Friday night closest to a full moon—to have a little bit of light in the dark—being the best night of the week to make our escape. We would sneak out as soon as everyone was in bed—and with no school or church the next day, it would give us just that little bit of extra time we didn't have the other days of the week when chores had to be done early. The only way out was to walk. What we would do after that, we had no idea. We didn't even know the geography around us, to be truthful.

"Maggie said, 'We're just gonna have to hope someone will pick up two girls needin' a ride.'

"It didn't occur to us then the risk that might entail with some man picking us up. We knew we had to travel light to travel fast. We left with the clothes on our backs, a little bag with a bar of soap, our tooth brushes, tooth paste and the $310 dollars I took from the barn. We were to a main road just as the sun was coming up.

"Maggie said, 'May this day bring some light into our lives.'

"She'd no sooner said that when an eighteen-wheeler pulled over and offered us a ride. We didn't think twice—we just climbed in. 'Where you two headed?' The man asked. Maggie asked, 'Where you headed?' He said, 'I've got to drive this load over to Boone, North Carolina.' Maggie said, 'That's where we were headin'.' I don't know if the truck driver believed that or not. She didn't know where Boone was and neither did I, but that's how we landed in Boone several hours later and have never left.

"We both got jobs washing dishes at restaurants, working double shifts as much as they'd let us, and lived pretty rough for a while trying to make that $310 last. Fortunately, our travels from the holler to Boone didn't cost us anything; in fact the nice truck driver even bought our breakfast. He suggested that he'd go in and get ours to go, as he wasn't sure it would be a good idea for him to go in with two young girls. That wouldn't have occurred to us but made sense when he said it.

"We bought a clunker car from someone who had one for sale in their front yard. Of course, we didn't even have driver's licenses but the man selling the car never asked, and we never said. Things were pretty loose in those days. We knew soon enough we were going to have to figure out how to get legal. If we had social security numbers or birth certificates we didn't know it. We were sure we didn't.

"We had a true-enough sob story that we were able to use those dedication certificates to get the ball rolling. I think it involved some sheriff in Tennessee having to go back to the holler and validate our 'shunning from the community.' I'm sure it also helped that we weren't the first to leave and that the sheriff knew exactly the problem. Maggie doubted he even went back there— that more likely he rubber-stamped the paperwork and was glad two more kids had escaped."

She concluded her account saying, "I guess it's kind of an amazing thing, but neither Maggie nor I ever cried before we left— during our first days free from that place or any day thereafter for the cards we'd been dealt."

Miles and I sat there dumbfounded. These two incredibly well-adjusted women had been through years we'd never imagined for them. I asked, "Have you ever run into anyone else from there or ever made any contact with your mothers?"

Ethel said, "We certainly both have pity for our mothers and any children who may still be caught up in that world, but there is no way either of us was would ever go back there to find out what it's like since we left. I'm not even sure we *could* find it. We have a general idea of where it is, but it would take some doing to find it again. Brother Sylvanus can't have lived forever, and we always hoped some kindlier person allowed the place to open up to the world."

I said, "Unfortunately there are too many Brother Sylvanuses in this world who use the Bible for a constant recitation of the few verses they find compelling."

Miles said, "With the men in your world as a child, I'm surprised you're so nice to us. I can see where you'd have nothing but hostility toward the male species."

She said, "I don't have to tell you that a couple of the men at the ol' boys' table down at the Daisy rub me the wrong way, but Maggie and I both felt such relief from our escape we never had any inkling of lumping all men in with that lot. In fact, that trucker was our first lifeline of many to follow until we found our way to a good and happy life."

We knew soon enough that Ethel had told Maggie of her disclosure of their past. One slow morning at the Daisy, Maggie came with our coffee and said, "I understand you two got the whole load from the holler to our landing in Boone. You didn't know we were that tough, did ya?"

I said, "We've always known you were tough. We just had no idea how you got that way, but we knew neither one of you got there by being a fool."

She laughed and said, "And now you know why neither one of us has ever been big churchgoers and are glad to work on Sunday mornings."

By now Ethel was standing there too. Miles said, "With Noel's story and you gals' story, it's really something you all three ended up working here together."

Ethel smiled and said, "You know how Noel likes to brag about taking the place of two. We like to kid him that it takes two tough gals to keep him in line and from getting the big head. And it must be said, we're family—and the only family I've got is Noel, Bob, Maggie and you two."

Maggie added, "And whether that man in the kitchen would ever say it or not, it's the only family he's got too."

When the reality of the circumstances of their lives sunk in, I realized just how true that was for the three of them. For me, once my parents were dead, our church friends dead or moved away, and Miles dead as well, they too were, for a time, the only family I really had anymore—that is, before an unlikely encounter with a young man and two boys from Macon, Georgia. They would expand my world and the worlds of Ethel, Maggie and Noel as well.

Chapter Forty-four

For some reason with our parents all dead, I decided to take on a project I should have done while they were living—for any light they might have been able to shed on it or interest they might have had in its findings. I started researching the Kilber (Kübler)-Shudel and the Bergeron-Savoie ancestry. It was a two-year project—though something I worked on and would set aside before tackling it again and again. My family tree was pretty easy, and the few lines that ended abruptly all ended in Switzerland or, in one case, Alsace. I quit when I got back to about the sixteenth century and decided there wasn't much point in doing any more. I never found anyone famous or infamous. No real surprises. There were some Ammans which made me wonder if Jacob Amman of the Amish faith might be a distant relative, but I never found any direct connection. There was also a Jung line which made me wonder if there could be any connection to Carl Jung and Elizabeth Kübler-Ross—both Swiss—but I didn't labor on these very hard as it was so distant as to be almost silly to try.

Miles' family was certainly interesting. From Louisiana things went in a pretty straight line back to Acadia—now Nova Scotia and New Brunswick—and back to France—more or less. While in Acadia, one of his direct ancestors married a woman from the Mi'kmaq Native American Tribe. In France, I soon discovered connections to aristocrats throughout France, Spain, Cyprus, Portugal and Italy. In fact, he was a direct descendent of Henry II of France, Catherine de Medici, and their daughter, Elizabeth and her husband Felipe, King of Spain and Portugal. The Savoies even had connections into Switzerland, and I told him on our next trip we we'd go to the family's old digs—Château de Chillon on Lake Geneva and Schloss Oberhöfen on Lake Thun. I've never been much for castle visits, but these are two we had planned to visit on our big trip together, and it amused us both greatly that Miles had direct ancestors who had resided there. Sadly, that was the trip I would take alone when it finally came.

I told him that what little I knew about Henry II and Catherine, explained to me where the ragin' part of the Cajun got into the family blood. There couldn't have been a starker contrast between my Mennonite roots and his aristocratic roots.

When we went back to Louisiana for the last time, when his oldest brother turned seventy, I had the Bergeron-Savoie family tree printed up on a vinyl banner which ran about 32 feet long and 4 feet high, and we hung it outside for everyone to see. We left it with the nephew who hosted the reunion for his dad.

I never did print up the Kibler-Shudel tree for myself, though I had pdf files of the "family book" and "family tree" that I sent to my sisters and as many cousins as I had email addresses for. I also sent it to the Grabers since it showed exactly how we were third cousins through the Shudels. It seemed like they were more interested than the nearer relatives.

It's hard to say exactly what value there is in such ancestry work. Certainly, some people like to find some connection to someone famous or even notorious. I expected neither in my family search and such was confirmed. I expected the same in Miles' tree and found surprise after surprise.

Perhaps one lesson—as you see the family lines fan out so quickly into names you had no idea were part of your history—is that defining oneself as a "Kibler" or a "Bergeron" is pretty meaningless. It is a label we use, but not one we should cling to as some kind of superior pedigree. My work certainly reinforced the egalitarian ethos I'd learned from my Swiss Mennonite roots. The "royal blood lines" that have defined so much of the power structures of our world look silly and trivial when viewed in the context of the breeding patterns of the human species. That may be my one true takeaway from all my work. For that lesson I'd have needed to look no further than David's exploitation of Saul's daughter Michal, Bathsheba and his other wives, and all the dysfunction that was passed from one generation to the next. All these millennia later, power still clings to superiority by bloodline and to my mind, it is vanity and all so much foolishness.

The night before Miles died, we saw on the news that Queen Elizabeth was getting ready to knight someone and he said, "At her age I hope she doesn't lose control of the sword and cut off the poor guy's head."

I laughed and said, "You do come up with some good ones every now and then." Then I said, "I doubt she has the strength to chop it off, but she might give him a good nick in the neck or take off an ear!" To which we both laughed.

I didn't know then that would be the last time we would laugh together. We watched TV that evening—not saying much. Most nights we didn't even say good night to each other. Sometimes I'd say, "Guten schlafen," and he'd say, "Bonne nuit." This was one of those nights we didn't say anything as we went to our rooms. The next morning, there he was in his bed with those rosary beads in his hand—dead.

Talking Politics at the Table

Chapter Forty-five

As is our normal pattern these days, whenever I get together with my "landlords" for a summer afternoon barbecue, we always meet up for a nice long visit well before when the meal is ready. This particular Saturday I was cooking. Johnny and Jimmy were off on their own bike adventures, and Tyler and Christian were sitting with me out on the patio.

Tyler said, "We've talked a lot about church and Christianity in general, but you've never waded much into day-to-day politics even though I know you keep up with such things. We all certainly share Momma Daisy and Pappy's firmness against war which I know you attribute to your own guides from your Mennonite upbringing. I know enough about you to not expect you to pick a partisan side and close your mind. I guess what I want to know is, have you ever considered yourself politically active?"

I said, "Well, if you want to know if I've ever marched in protest and got locked up as a consequence, the answer is simple enough; no, I have not. I can admire those who have, given the precursor that they live their lives consistent with what they protest against. You would think that is an obvious given, but it rarely is."

Christian, who had moved to a firmness against war by his association with the Jemison legacy, piped in, "I can't help but think of Thomas Merton who said what hypocrites we are when we arm ourselves to the teeth and use war as our remedy all the while praying for peace. As he put it, it's like praying for good health and drinking poison the whole time."

"We drink a lot of poison in this country," I said. "Merton, King, the Berrigan brothers—we had plenty of strong Christian voices speaking powerfully against the war and yet the evil prevailed. It is depressing.

"It is a sad thing to say, but any honest assessment would have to confirm that since I first could vote in an election, every single president, senator and congressman has been an abject failure to my values. Some I voted for in hope that they might rise above the

191

election rhetoric and actually be a statesman for the common good of all—here and abroad. They were always a great disappointment. Some I expected to be as bad as I could imagine and they managed to even supersede my low expectation of them."

Christian asked, "Do you care to name names?"

"No," I said, "I have never been inclined in that manner as it's too easy for the hearer to make assumptions of how my politics align with theirs—and thus only serves to either validate in their mind how 'right' they are or how 'wrong' I am. I certainly don't think such would be the case with you two, but I also believe we are able to look beyond the personalities to the real core issues. Such being the case, the latest name on the ballot is just that—the stand-in for the power brokers of this country.

"I have, over the years, written to my congressmen, senators and even presidents. If I get a response, I can predict in advance what it is going to say. Some prewritten form letter will thank me for contacting their office, and tell me why they are right and how my inferior mind clearly can't grasp the importance of spending endlessly on security and defense. Why the latest war is a battle for our democracy. I certainly have seen it doesn't matter the degree of thoughtfulness I put into my letter—it is dismissed out of hand. At most, no more than a check mark in the column 'lunatic fringe' where they tally how their constituents line up in support of them.

"The press is no help and only getting worse every year. For decades I have listened to them use the tired justification, 'analysts say' and 'sources suggest.' Report the facts and get some evidence! Sources suggest Santa Claus exists. Oh well then, it must true! That may sound absurd, but we've gone to war on just these kinds of ridiculous assertions—complete fabrications used to justify another war for profit. And of course it's not just war—it is all manner of power, greed and exploitation. All too often war serves as the primary distraction for all else."

Tyler said, "This is one of those conversations when I wish Momma and Pappy could be here to join in. I am always astounded by how we, as southern Blacks, and you as a midwestern Mennonite could arrive at such a remarkable kinship of mind—if that's the right thing to call it."

"That term works for me," I said.

Christian added, "I think it's a kinship of grace which I realize is a term a lot of people toss around but don't really understand. Dietrich Bonhoeffer certainly understood the notion of what passes for grace for so many—cheap grace as he put."

Tyler added, "Religion by legalism."

Then Tyler asked, "What do we say to the Johnnys and Jimmys of the world who are told in school about the evils of the Hitlers of the world and how we needed war to stop them?"

"Well, first let me say, I do wish I could have met your momma and pappy. I know you know that, but sometimes I actually *long* for it. I just have to remind myself that you and Uncle Ira are their stand-ins for my benefit."

Then I said, "You probably can guess my first response to that kind of question. If that's the only way your history teacher can read history, then you need to find a better teacher or go off and educate yourself. To drill in just one layer deep—and there are many layers to examine—I'm hard-pressed to see in history how World War I wasn't the complete folly of Queen Victoria's offspring run amuck. And with the Versailles Treaty that ended that mess, the seeds were planted to give Hitler's brand of nationalism all the shit it needed to flourish. From there, we drug ourselves into Korea and the rice paddies of Vietnam. War begets war. The Old Testament prophets recognized it then, and we continue to ignore them to our peril."

I excused myself to go get the vegetables out of the refrigerator. When I opened the door, I thought of something I wanted to read to them that they might get a kick out of. I reached out the patio door and said, "Christian, check the meat and put these on the grill. I wanna grab something. I'll be right back."

The boys were just getting back from their bike adventures around the neighborhood. They each grabbed an orange LaCroix and joined their dads on the patio.

When I got back Christian said, "I think I'll take the meat off to rest and turn the grill low to just keep the veggies warm."

"Sounds like a plan," I said.

Hearing the boys come in, I printed off five copies of what it was that I went to get. Before I handed it to them I said, "When Trump was elected I wrote him a letter as though the ghost of

Lincoln was writing to him. I'll read it to you but wanted you to see the parts that are direct quotes from Lincoln which are in italics."

The Inaugural Letter, January 20, 2017
Dear President D. Trump:

Every four years my spirit is moved to write to the newly sworn in president to share my thoughts on presidential leadership. If they happen to be returning for another term, then this letter pertains to my assessment of their leadership during the previous term. As this is your first term, you will get the standard first-term advice adjusted for inflation or deflation according to the times at hand.

In your case, it is decidedly the inflation-adjusted letter. Egos being what they are, this is usually the case. At least you don't seem to make any attempt to mask it in some pseudo humility as most do. Don't take this as a compliment. I see no virtue in your boasting. *What kills a skunk is the publicity it gives itself. I hold that while man exists, it is his duty to improve not only his own condition, but to assist in ameliorating mankind.*

You may sleep in "my bed" for the novelty because you can as the current tenant of that so-called house of the people, but I hope more assuredly you will walk a bit in my shoes.

While I write in hope, always, it must be acknowledged that few take my advice. Most defy it outright while paying homage to me as a great president. Martin Luther King, Jr., one of the great American prophets, certainly comprehended the problems and the solutions as I would lay them out.

To that end, *I should like to know if, taking this old Declaration of Independence, which declares that all men are equal upon principle, you begin making exceptions to it, where will you stop? If one man says it does not mean a Negro, why not another say it does not mean some other man* (a Muslim)?

I don't mind saying about my presidency that sometimes I wish I had let the South go their own way. One can dream that their problems might have been their own and my own northern kinship might have been somehow better.

Yes, I know this is highly unlikely. Interconnected complicity being what it is. Abuse of power and privilege being what they are. *As I have not felt, so I have not expressed any harsh sentiment towards our Southern brethren. I have constantly declared, as I really believed, the only difference between them and us is the difference of circumstances.*

More than ever, you are presiding over a country that is interconnected to other nations. We have made many of these connections destructive. *It is not my nature, when I see a people borne down by the weight of their shackles — the oppression of tyranny — to make their life more bitter by heaping upon them greater burdens; but rather would I do all in my power to raise the yoke than to add anything that would tend to crush them.*

We have crushed many. We have allowed the economy to blindly and audaciously exploit. *These capitalists generally act harmoniously and in concert to fleece the people; and now that they have got into a quarrel with themselves, we are called upon to appropriate the people's money to settle the quarrel.*

It has so happened in all ages of the world that some have labored, and others have, without labor, enjoyed a large proportion of the fruits. We have become the great task master of this economic injustice. *The man who could go to Africa and rob her of her children, and then sell them into interminable bondage, with no other motive than that which is furnished by dollars and cents, is so much worse than the most depraved murderer that he can never receive pardon at my hand.*

For the past fifty years, virtually every president has managed to preside over ever more vitriolic internal hostility that sadly is exported to unsuspecting poor in nations around the globe. You did not cause this, though again adjusting for inflation, I fear you will perpetuate it.

This is yours to do to prove me wrong. Please do!

Our defense is in the preservation of the spirit which prizes liberty as a heritage of all men, in all lands, everywhere. Destroy this spirit and you have planted the seeds of despotism around your own doors.

This nation has lost any vision of unity. I am sickened by its red and blue state duality. These are not *the better angels of our nature. If the great American people will only keep their temper, on both sides of the line, the troubles will come to an end, and the question which now distracts the country will be settled just as surely as all other difficulties of* like character which have originated in this government have been adjusted.

I was a man who honored vows however inconvenient—both my marriage vows and my vows to preserve, protect and defend the Union. Certainly, neither Union nor my wife were easy partnerships. They had much in common. They would harass me. Insult me. Demand more from me than I should have had to give.

The deaths in my home and in my country would bear down upon me with unrelenting force. I presided over the darkest days of our history. I saved the Union. I helped set a course to free a race of human beings. But these mean nothing if I was not able to feel remorse for not finding a better way. I believed these failures of war would require my atonement.

The gunman did his worst. The President of the Union had died as the insurrection had made him live. While this may have been a just end for me, it brought no just way forward for our nation. The nation squandered the freed slaves' liberty and denied their dignity. This is a sin not wholly redeemed to this day. Reconciliation is needed now in great measure.

I have always found that mercy bears richer fruits than strict justice. Those who deny freedom to others deserve it not for themselves; and under the rule of a just God, cannot long retain it.

That our presidents have failed to learn the greatest lesson I taught remains the tragedy of our common history. The dead shall die in vain so long as our presidents, remorseless, make war for profit and levy cruel sanctions because they can; and instead of atonement for their own redemption and ours, defend imaginary legacies, write memoirs and build presidential libraries to their greatness. This is not greatness. This is vanity.

I want it said of me by those who knew me best, that I always plucked a thistle and planted a flower where I thought a flower would grow.

You are the forty-fifth man to have an opportunity to chart a course of mercy and healing for a nation that continues to allow the war machine to define this Union. Can you *bind up the wounds* of this nation and *care for its widow,* for *its orphan* and oppressed and all those it oppresses? It is no small thing to ask.

It is this thing a great president must be willing to try, and to humbly seek redemption for where he fails. May you defy all odds and be a president *of the people, by the people and for the people* for the sake of all humanity and the poor of every nation. *America will never be destroyed from the outside. If we falter and lose our freedoms, it will be because we destroyed ourselves.*

Yours respectfully,

A Lincoln

PS   *A private soldier has as much right to justice as a major-general.* Beware of taking the advice of generals.

I put the letter down and got up to get dinner on the table. I'd no more stood up when Johnny said, "He didn't seem to take Mr. Lincoln's advice."

Christian said, "Maybe if you or your brother ever become president you can be the first to do so."

Realizing the gravity of such an idea, Tyler added, "That very notion feels like an immeasurable weight. I'm not sure I could bear even the thought of it for our boys."

I reassured Tyler in some small measure, "Well until it happens, let's enjoy each other unencumbered with such a weight and carry the one we must bear today. That is burden enough."

Life never felt like much of a burden when I was around the Marvel-Jemisons. They kept my funk at bay and quickly enough brought me out of my frequent melancholy moods. We ate our dinner with a delightful recounting of the boys watching frogs they had discovered in the nearby creek—as the frogs would eat bugs off the water's surface and other simple pleasures of their journey that afternoon.

The next Saturday it was the Marvel-Jemisons who hosted our afternoon barbecue. The boys were off on another adventure, and we picked up where we had left off the Saturday before.

Tyler said, "I spent the week going through history backwards, the same way Momma Daisy always recounted anyone you happened to ask her about."

"One of her many endearing traits, I've always thought," I interjected.

Tyler continued, "As you suggested about war begetting war, I worked my way back and never could find a real end. It does seem to hold as a near absolute that, for different reasons but all true enough, one begets the next."

"A rather depressing thought," Christian said.

I added, "And yet one that suggests how little it would take if people actually labored for peace as hard as they connive for power and greed. Somehow we have to break the notion of being warriors for a cause and embrace a peaceable language that looks for what *can* be instead of what *must* be. I know, I'm a broken record, though I guess that is an archaism the boys wouldn't understand and you may even be too young to understand."

Christian said, "We're not that young. We know what a broken record is—a broken record is—a broken record is—a broken record is."

"Cute," I said smiling back at his quick comeback.

Tyler said, "Isn't it sad that all our politicians claim to be good Christians, and yet somehow their practice looks nothing like what our family heritage could even remotely recognize as their faith?"

"It is heartbreaking," I said. "The result is we fight to claw our way to some new 'right' that is just an infant step toward the call of dignity for all—trying to make two tiny steps forward for every giant step back. But the problem is, these become objects to toss around, ignore or discard according to time, place, power and money. These are the uneven scales of injustice at work."

Christian said, "I'm in sympathy with Lincoln—when I'm gone let it be said of me of those who knew me best, I planted a flower where I thought one would grow."

"That one thought has connotations for a lot of pondering on how we live our lives," Tyler reflected.

I added, "Along with those words my grandfather carved over Hope Mennonite's doors—Loving God, Loving Ourselves, Loving Others—one has an ethos that is about as good as the human species can realize. I have to say though, I do take issue with Mr. Lincoln on pulling up a thistle to plant a flower. There are quite a few thistles I find rather beautiful and have nearly always let them be. But I know what he meant and appreciate the longing for beauty his sentiment invokes."

Christian laughed and said, "Now I know why that big thistle survives back there in the dog cemetery."

I said, "That's right—now you know!"

Such thoughts made the three of us just want to get up and wander around the garden—and enjoy the beds of daisies and salvia and holly-hocks, the odd weed or thistle I leave because I like them, and stroll through the rose garden set ablaze in color with their rich fragrance filling our senses.

We'd had enough of politics and religion for a while. It was time to "just be."

Chapter Forty-six

On one of my more rare church visits these past years, I decided to drive myself out to Valle Crucis. Christian's folks were in town and Christian had talked to the rector about allowing his mom to preach. I beat them there and went to my usual pew. Christian's dad sat in the pew with me and the Marvel-Jemisons were in the row right behind. Christian's brother, Giles, had graduated and moved on by then so we only saw him on rare occasions.

Instead of trying to get our group into the Daisy on a noisy, busy Sunday, we'd decided beforehand to come to my place for lunch. I had things ready that we could just pull out of the fridge and put together quickly. Tyler had picked up two mincemeat pies from the Daisy on Saturday "for old times sake."

I had said when he dropped them by, "I don't guess one piece will kill me. It's been a long time since I've had Noel's good mincemeat."

It was one of those Sundays where the hymns were okay but none I was all that fond of. Christian's dad apparently had the same thoughts as I that morning. He said, "I don't have anything against number 10 in the hymnal but I'd have preferred if they'd picked number 9 which is one of my favorites."

I knew exactly what number 9 was—*Morning Song* with words by Studdert-Kennedy. It too is one of my favorites.

Then he proceeded to sing the entire hymn.

Not here for high and holy things
we render thanks to thee,
but for the common things of earth,
the purple pageantry
of dawning and of dying days,
the splendor of the sea,

the royal robes of autumn moors,
the golden gates of spring,
the velvet of soft summer nights,
the silver glistering
of all the million million stars,

200

the silent song they sing,

of faith and hope and love undimmed,
undying still through death,
the resurrection of the world,
what time there comes the breath
of dawn that rustles through the trees,
and that clear voice that saith:

Awake, awake to love and work!
The lark is in the sky,
the fields are wet with diamond dew,
the worlds awake to cry
their blessings on the Lord of life,
as he goes meekly by.

Come, let thy voice be one with theirs,
shout with their shout of praise;
see how the giant sun soars up,
great lord of years and days!
So let the love of Jesus come
and set thy soul ablaze,

to give and give, and give again,
what God hath given thee;
to spend thyself nor count the cost;
to serve right gloriously
the God who gave all worlds that are,
and all that are to be.

"I just love that," he said. Then he said to Johnny and Jimmy, "You probably don't know the story about the man who wrote those words, do you?"

Jimmy said, "We do if his name was Horatio Spafford."

"You sure do know about that man," he answered. "No, this man was Geoffrey Anketell Studdert-Kennedy. Isn't that a mouthful? He was an Anglican priest and volunteered to serve as a chaplain during World War I. He earned the nickname, Woodbine

Willie, because he would always carry a pack of Woodbine cigarettes for soldiers who were wounded and wanted a smoke. He was awarded the Military Cross for running into no man's land on the front lines to rescue wounded soldiers. After the war he became an outspoken critic of war and wrote several books. The first one he called simply, *Lies*. Another was *The Church Is Not a Movement but a Mob*. He didn't hold back as you can see just from those two titles.

Johnny said, "Woodbine Willie—I like that nickname."

Tyler said, "Don't get any ideas about taking up smoking out of admiration for the name."

Jimmy snickered and said, "Woodbine Johnny."

I said, "I'm glad to hear you tell the boys the good priest's story. It would suit me if we sang number 9 at least once a month. The short time I led services when we were without a priest, I did my best to make sure the congregation knew that hymn and sang it like they meant it—which I believe some did. Certainly Miles and I did.

"There was a song in the Church of God hymnal that didn't make it into the Episcopal hymnal. When I was leading services, I had the words printed in the bulletin. It was set to the beautiful tune *Finlandia*. Too bad Miles isn't here. He liked to sing solos. I never did, but I guess I can try this one time. The first two verses were written by an American who ran off to join the circus when he was a boy." I figured this little known fact would get the boys' attention, which it did. Then I sang the verses he wrote.

This is my song, oh God of all the nations,
a song of peace for lands afar and mine.
This is my home, the country where my heart is;
here are my hopes, my dreams, my holy shrine;
but other hearts in other lands are beating
with hopes and dreams as true and high as mine.

My country's skies are bluer than the ocean,
and sunlight beams on clover leaf and pine.
But other lands have sunlight, too, and clover,
and skies are everywhere as blue as mine.
This is my song, thou God of all the nations;
a song of peace for their land and for mine.

We were all standing around in the kitchen as we were putting lunch together but in no hurry to get it done. Then I said, "The next verse was by Josh Mitteldorf who I can't tell you much about. I like it since it so aptly tells how we get sucked into supporting war." Then I sang verse three.

When nations rage, and fears erupt coercive,
the drumbeats sound, invoking pious cause.
My neighbors rise, their stalwart hearts they offer,
the gavels drop, suspending rights and laws.
While others wield their swords with blind devotion;
for peace I'll stand, my true and steadfast cause.

"Finally, I added a verse from the Universalist hymnal to wrap it all up."
We would be one, as now we join in singing
our hymn of love, to pledge ourselves anew.
To that high cause of greater understanding
of who we are, and what in us is true.
We would be one in loving and forgiving,
with hopes and dreams as true and high as thine.

Christian's mom said, "That really ought to be in the hymnal. I want to get those words and use it for the Sunday closest to July 4th and a few other Sundays throughout the year—we can always use inspiration when it comes to peace."

I wasn't quite done yet. "Since my churchgoin' days, I've added two more verses—more personal reflection than intended for a congregation. I call them my epitaph."

A dawn shall rise when peace prevails forever.
All wars have ceased, and tribal strife's no more.
I'll see anew, the beauty that surrounds us,
in humble thanks for all our world has given.
When in my heart all truth is gently beating,
my life's last breath is one with Thee, my Friend.

This is my end, and so my Just beginning.

I know not how my death shall bring new life.
What peace I've known, I've known was grace perfected,
as you, my Friend, have led me on my way.
Your mercy—great; your steadfast love has held me
and, thus, has healed me for the dawn of peace.

Lunch was all set up now and ready. Tyler said, "With those hymns, I think we've said our grace," adding, "and all the people said,..."

And we all responded, "Amen."

What Was and Is

Epilogue

I've been a little surprised how few people have had any meaningful connection to me, including most of my own siblings, aunts, uncles and cousins. I don't feel any particular estrangement from them but not any closeness either. I was thinking about how neither Tyler nor Ira talked about the generation before Momma Daisy and Pappy. Momma and Pappy were such tremendous forces in their lives—surely the ones who came before them must have had remarkable stories to tell. It seems very difficult to pass these stories from generation to generation, though thankfully we do latch onto certain guides who show us the way. I count it a great blessing that what may be lacking in breadth never lacked depth. The depth and richness of the most influential in my life are pure gifts. I never did anything to deserve all the love poured down upon me.

As I reflect on all the changes I've seen over the few short decades of my life, there is much to be grateful for and much to lament. Perhaps the books balance, but the lamentation side of the register seems pretty heavy at times.

When I look back to our family farms, and the 150 years over which they were built and during which they supported our families, they are now largely relics of a bygone era. Many barns sit empty. Some have been sold off for their good timber—at least ensuring a third life, first as a tree in the forest, second as a fine barn that provided a family with their food and income, and now some other building—perhaps a home, or a restaurant, or both in the case of bigger barns.

There are those like Bob and Deb who maintain their barn for the sake of appearance and nostalgia. Many tore down the old farmhouses and built bigger homes for smaller families—each with three- or four-car garages.

Too many old barns stand in complete neglect as the leaky roofs slowly cause the grand old structures to fall in on themselves—now just dangerous piles of wood awaiting a match to put them out of their misery. The fields are joined into bigger fields with most all of the woods gone, and little to no crop diversity. Everything is dependent on fuels, chemicals, processes food manufacturers and volatile foreign markets—and it must be said, "corporate welfare."

In more recent years, some of the land the farmers had tried to crop finally went back to wetlands and became property of the government through a buy-back program. This might be one credit on the other side of the column, but not one that can outweigh all the debits to progress that come through an extractive and military economy.

As the orchards aged, they too were bulldozed and turned into more tillable acreage. Why bother with a fruit tree when you can get it all year-round at the grocery store?

Now, the large gardens of my childhood are just acres of grass maintained with their zero-turn mowers that cost more than a tractor did in my childhood days. Many make the effort to keep nice trees and flower beds. Plenty just leave old stumps of the cut down, dead trees or leave dead trees standing where the only green is the Virginia creeper that took over their old branches. Now, they stand lifeless waiting for some storm to topple them over. Places where the barns are gone and the trees are gone look like desolate, unloved habitations of their indifferent occupants.

"Progress" even came to Hope Mennonite in the early 2000s when it was decided they should be on a main road, close to town, and have more of an "auditorium-style worship space" where they could "grow the church."

When I told Miles about this he said, "I hope I don't puke."

I said, "Perhaps the more generous response would be to say, 'It's not our cup of tea.'"

To that notion he said, "I hope I don't puke," adding, "Your Grandma Shudel would be boxing the ears of any of those still there who are distant relatives of hers."

With that I replied, "Given her love for Hope Mennonite, she'd be boxing their ears related or not!"

With the new building going up, the church council even voted to leave the Mennonite conference and join a loose group of evangelical churches. They certainly didn't want to maintain the old Hope Mennonite building for anything, and so they had it torn down. If anyone rescued the carving above the door, I never knew it. I hope someone did. Both my sisters married Lutherans and no longer went to Hope so they didn't see to it. If there was one thing I'd like to think survived the wrecking ball and bulldozer, it would be that.

I was a little surprised that they didn't make some effort to save the timber frame rather than have it all go to the county landfill—but I guess since no money could be realized from its sale, it was just more trouble than any were willing to give it when destroying it all was quicker and easier. The way the Kiblers and Shudels deeded the land, they had to give it away. Otherwise, I'm sure the council and "elders" would have sold the church site to the highest bidder—the cemetery and former church land was given to the township to maintain the entire plot as a cemetery as the deed prescribed should it no longer be used as a church.

Now, only the dead bear witness to the community of faith that was once the center of so many lives in the township.

I won't be buried there. My ashes will be interred back home in the dog cemetery with Miles. But one thing Miles and I did do once the old church came down was add a simple stone monument out by the road. It read simply—

Loving God
Loving Ourselves
Loving Others

The two of us stood just off the old township road in front of the monument as we looked past it, past the many headstones of my family and neighbors, past the trees that now shaded the graves—most of which I planted as a boy and have grown large—and onto what were the Kibler and Shudel homesteads that once thrived there—now only large cornfields. Miles saw tears running down my cheeks.

I said to him, "No, I'm not weeping for what might have been or what I believe still should be. I weep for what was and for what those gentle people instilled in my soul."

www.ingramcontent.com/pod-product-compliance
Lightning Source LLC
Chambersburg PA
CBHW030754210626
46807CB00017B/2474